FIGHTING FANTASY

APPOINTMENT
—— WITH ——
F.E.A.R.

STEVE JACKSON

■SCHOLASTIC

Scholastic Children's Books
An imprint of Scholastic Ltd
Euston House, 24 Eversholt Street, London, NW1 1DB, UK
Registered office: Westfield Road, Southam, Warwickshire, CV47 0RA
SCHOLASTIC and associated logos are trademarks and/or
registered trademarks of Scholastic Inc.

First published in the UK by Penguin Group, 1985
This edition by Scholastic Ltd, 2018

ISBN 978 1 407 18617 7

A CIP catalogue record for this book
is available from the British Library.

Printed by CPI Group (UK) Ltd, Croydon, CR0 4YY
Papers used by Scholastic Children's Books are made
from wood grown in sustainable forests.

1 3 5 7 9 10 8 6 4 2

www.scholastic.co.uk

CONTENTS

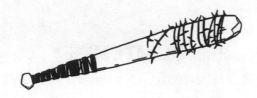

HOW WILL YOU START
YOUR ADVENTURE?

The book you hold in your hands is a gateway to another world – a world of astonishing superpowers, radioactive beasts, deadly cyborgs, terrifying super-villains and a city in peril. Welcome to the world of **FIGHTING FANTASY!**

You are about to embark upon a thrilling fantasy adventure in which **YOU** are the hero! **YOU** decide which route to take, which dangers to risk and which creatures to fight. But be warned – it will also be **YOU** who has to live or die by the consequences of your actions.

Take heed, for success is by no means certain, and you may well fail in your mission on your first attempt. But have no fear, for with experience, skill and luck, each new attempt should bring you a step closer to your ultimate goal.

Prepare yourself, for when you turn the page you will enter an exciting, perilous **FIGHTING FANTASY** adventure where every choice is yours to make, an adventure in which **YOU ARE THE HERO!**

How would you like to begin your adventure?

IF YOU ARE NEW TO FIGHTING FANTASY ...

It's a good idea to read through the rules which appear on pages 257-265 before you start.

IF YOU HAVE PLAYED FIGHTING FANTASY BEFORE ...

You'll realize that to have any chance of success, you will need to discover your hero's attributes. You can create your own character by following the instructions on pages 257–259. Make sure you also read the rules on Super Powers and Clues on pages 8-12, and on Hero Points on page 264. Don't forget to enter your character's details on the Adventure Sheet which appears on page 266 .

SUPER POWERS AND CLUES

You are Jean Lafayette, the product of a dangerous – but successful – genetic experiment. Although seemingly normal as a child, it became apparent in your early teens that you were a far from ordinary human being. You are gifted with a superhuman power, which you have sworn to use only for the benefit of your fellow man. As the Silver Crusader, you are well known to the population of Titan City. Most people admire you, some distrust you, but *all* members of the underworld fear you. Only your parents, who are both dead, ever knew your real identity and the origin of your powers.

In the adventures ahead, you will begin with one of four powers. During your daily activities and encounters with disasters and super-criminals, you will have two objectives. First, you must learn the whereabouts of the secret meeting of F.E.A.R. (the Federation of Euro-American Rebels) which is due to take place within the next few days. This dangerous alliance of master-criminals and enemy agents is planning to overthrow the governments of the western world and establish their own rule. Secondly, you may assess your own performance as a superhero by trying to gain as many Hero Points as possible.

Before you start each adventure, you may choose which super power to start with, from the four powers listed below. You will also start the game with knowledge of two clues. Following the description of each super power, you will find instructions on where to find your clues, which are hidden in the text of the adventure. Before you turn to reference 1 to start your adventure, choose your super power, locate and read the clues and enter the information on your *Adventure Sheet*.

SUPER STRENGTH

You have the strength of many men. The muscles of your immensely powerful legs and arms bulge through the fabric of your costume. They are developed to the point of perfection and, in combat situations, you always fight with a *SKILL* of 13. You also have the power to fly through the air at any speed you wish. This allows you to hover unsupported above the ground or to chase and catch up with the fastest jet.

To find the first of your clues, turn to reference **127**. For your other clue, you may choose one from the following:

108   **280**   **312**

PSI-POWERS

You have extraordinary mental abilities. You are able to reach into the thoughts of most other humans (and some animals) to read their minds and influence them. You also have limited powers to make objects move mentally and even to change the very nature of some elements. However, using this power is an enormous mental effort for you. Each time you use your *Psi-Power,* you must deduct 2 *STAMINA* points.

Turn to **222** to discover your first clue. You may also choose one clue from the following:

280   **152**   **108**

ENHANCED TECHNOLOGICAL SKILL (ETS)

Your considerable intelligence has allowed you to develop a whole collection of hi-tech gadgetry. Through advanced micro-circuitry designs, you have been able to miniaturize most of these gadgets so that they will fit conveniently into a special Accessory Belt worn around your waist. Whatever the situation, you are usually fortunate enough to have something appropriate to use. However, you have avoided developing weaponry in case any weapon you developed should ever fall into the wrong hands and be used by the criminal element to wreak untold havoc.

You start the adventure with two clues, which must be chosen from the following list:

280   **88**   **152**

ENERGY BLAST

You are able to summon up electrostatic energy from within your own body and channel it out through your fingertips. You can aim these Energy Bolts at adversaries or objects and your control is such that you know before you aim how much force will be needed to deal with them. You have taken a personal oath that you will only stun any *human* target, no matter how villainous your opponent may be. When using *Energy Blast,* you need only determine whether or not your aim is true; if you hit a human opponent, the effect will be an automatic stun. Test your aim by rolling two dice. If the result is *equal to or less than* your *SKILL* score, the Bolt has hit. If the result is *higher than* your *SKILL,* you have missed and a normal battle must be fought or the situation must be resolved as per the instructions in the text. Sometimes you will not be able to use a second Bolt. Each time you use *Energy Blast,* you must deduct 2 *STAMINA* points.

Your first clue will be found at reference **88**. For your second clue, you may choose one of the following:

222   **312**   **280**

BACKGROUND

The time of your birth was an anxious moment for your parents and their doctors. Your mother had consented to undergo an experimental form of genetic surgery. The doctors had warned her of the dangers of the radiation experiments; their research programme was nowhere near complete. But this she already knew, for she herself was one of the researchers. The work had reached the stage where progress was impossible without testing it on a human subject. Your father had not fully understood the implications when he gave his consent, and eight pairs of apprehensive eyes watched your arrival into the world.

Their first reaction was one of relief. You certainly seemed a normal, healthy baby. Post-natal tests showed no physical deformities whatsoever. In fact, you appeared to be a fine specimen. In your younger years your development was carefully monitored with a seemingly endless series of physiological and psychological tests, all of which you passed with flying colours. The doctors and researchers congratulated themselves; their experiments were a complete success. However, the experiments had been conducted in a shroud of secrecy. Had the world known of the risks of the experiment, public outcry would have been overwhelming. It would certainly have put an end to further genetic research. And from your mother's point of view, she had no wish to have the world regard you as an experimental freak. Only a few knew what had really happened.

Over the years, the testing stopped as the doctors felt more and more certain that there was no need to monitor your progress. As fate would have it, it was just when this testing *stopped* that it became clear that you were anything but a normal child. Your latent superhuman powers did not show themselves until after the doctors had lost interest.

Your parents, who had become thoroughly fed up with the endless tests, decided that your extraordinary powers must remain a secret from the world. They had no wish to have you studied as some kind of freak for the rest of your life.

You have a regular job working in an office of a medium-sized company. But when duty calls, you become the Silver Crusader, upholder of justice; and you have taken an oath to serve in the fight against crime in Titan City. Apart from your own super abilities, you have one other device to aid you – your Crimewatch. This neat little device, worn around your wrist, receives and broadcasts transmissions to and from your two most important allies. You can be contacted by police headquarters through this Crimewatch and you can also summon the police to aid you. In addition, your friend and underworld contact Gerry the Grass is able to warn you of impending crimes through the Crimewatch.

Gerry the Grass has recently become aware of an important meeting about to take place within the next few days. Vladimir Utoshski, leader of F.E.A.R. (the Federation of Euro-American Rebels), has been summoning his aides-in-crime to meet in Titan City. Utoshski, also known as the Titanium Cyborg, is a super-villain whose field of expertise is the electronic enhancement of human abilities. He is part man, part machine – and very dangerous. Gerry the Grass has not yet found out where or when the meeting is due, but one thing is certain. Its purpose is to finalize plans for a scheme which would mean disaster for the western world. The meeting must be stopped! You must find out where and when this meeting is due to take place and prevent it at all costs...

MAY YOUR STAMINA NEVER FAIL!

NOW TURN OVER...

You can't help but feel that something is not quite right

As you walk the ten blocks to work that morning, you can't help but feel that something is not quite right. You stop by a telephone booth to consider what it could be.

The sounds of the city are the usual 8 a.m. cacophony. Cars and buses bounce past along Clark Street, their drivers too sleepy even to try to avoid the pits and bumps in the road. A newspaper-vendor bawls an incomprehensible headline – something about a robbery – at the crowds of men and women milling past him on their ways to work. Overhead in the sky the rhythmic beating of a traffic 'copter's blades fades into the distance. An argument is taking place between an elderly businessman and an over-large woman with an untrained dog, whose sidewalk deposits have offended the businessman. There is nothing unusual ... or is there?

The difference is only barely perceptible, but there is a distinct air of tension in the streets. There are nervous twitches in the eyes of the passers-by; the cars are accelerating and braking in a jittery manner – little things like that. To your heightened senses, the atmosphere is pregnant. Today will not be just another day.

Your thoughts are broken by the high-pitched wailing of a police siren. A yellow and black Cougar GS screeches round the corner and leaps ahead through the Clark Street traffic before swinging left into Audubon Park. Behind it, the traffic settles back into its regular flow. Your attention drifts back to the argument. A small crowd has built up around the man and woman. Raised voices are taking one side or the other and the situation is beginning to look nasty. What will you do next:

Go over and see if you can break up
the argument?   Turn to **263**

Run after the police car into
Audubon Park?   Turn to **289**

Buy a newspaper to find out about
the robbery?   Turn to **228**

Ignore all these incidents and go to work?   Turn to **341**

2

You manage to seal the lid on the crate, thus trapping the creature that was Mustapha Kareem. Kareem's jacket fell off the Mummy's shoulders as you hurled it into the crate and now lies on the ground. You pick it up and rummage through the pockets. You find two pieces of paper inside. One bears the emblem of F.E.A.R. and you unfold it quickly. The bottom half of the paper is ripped off, but the message reads: 'Meeting in executive jet...' The second piece of paper is a scribbled note which simply says 'Crate', followed by an Egyptian hieroglyphic character. You check the crates in the room. One bears a symbol identical to that on the note. Inside are a number of pieces of gold jewellery which match those on the main exhibit! Kareem had been stealing these and replacing them with imitations! Having now exposed the fraud, you may hand the affair over to the police. Award yourself 4 Hero Points and turn to **276**.

3

You hide behind the gate until Bronski is close. When you can hear his footsteps approaching, you spring out to confront him. The startled killer reaches into his coat and pulls out a weapon: a battery-powered electric knife! Resolve your combat with him:

'CHAINSAW' BRONSKI   SKILL 8   STAMINA 8

If you manage to defeat him, turn to **93**.

4

You arrive at the circus as preparations are being made for the evening's performance. Caravans are clustered around the huge big top and round the back are the animal cages. A dwarf dressed in a clown's outfit comes running over to you as you arrive. He cannot talk, but instead honks a bicycle horn excitedly, grabs your hand and pulls. He seems to want you to follow him. Will you follow him as he wishes (turn to **399**)? Or will you head for the lion cages (turn to **310**) or an important-looking caravan in the centre (turn to **223**)?

5

You try valiantly to smash the door. But your efforts are futile against so solid a door. Your best plan would have been not to waste your strength on this door, because in trying to smash it, you injure yourself. Deduct 1 *SKILL* and 2 *STAMINA* points (if your power is *Super Strength,* deduct only 2 *STAMINA* points). Turn now to **60**.

6

How will you escape from your prison? There seems to be only one plan open to you. You will have to use a bolt of energy to blast through the door. But the door is ten centimetres of solid metal! Its weak spot must be the small glass window set in the door. You prepare yourself and unleash a controlled blast. The glass turns from red to yellow as it melts. The heat inside the chamber is tremendous, but a welcome rush of cool air hits your face as the glass drops away. There is just enough room for you to reach out and grasp the handle to release yourself. With great relief, you step out into the corridor. Voices are coming from behind a door at the far end of the passage and you step up, ready for action. Turn to **298**.

7

You fight your way through the crowd until you reach a spot where you can just about see the cars arrive up the avenue over the heads of the crowd in front of you.

Twenty minutes later, the cavalcade arrives and cheers go up from the crowd. As the President's car approaches, you catch sight of a man in front of you struggling with something. His hand comes free – he is holding a gun and is preparing to point it at the President! You are in your street clothes and cannot use your super powers, but you must do something to prevent the man getting a shot at the President. You leap on him from behind:

ASSASSIN   *SKILL 7*   *STAMINA 6*

After the second round of combat, turn to **359**.

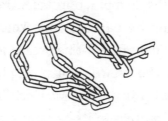

8

You grab the little thief by his shoulder and turn him round, telling him that he must not steal; he must work hard and *earn* the money he needs to buy what he wants. A sneer breaks out across the boy's face and he reaches into his pocket as if to get the Munchie Bars. But when his hand comes out it is gripping a loaded pistol! His sneer changes to a sly smile as he pulls the trigger and, from this range, he cannot miss. Your life as a superhero is over. . .

You establish line-of-sight with the man and woman in the centre of the crowd and concentrate. As your powers take effect, their argument dwindles and ceases. They look around in astonishment at the crowd which has built up. The woman shrugs her shoulders and walks off with her dog. The man looks towards you and freezes. Keeping your *Psi-Powers* focused on him for as long as you are able, you realize this man is not as he appears. He is desperately trying to keep from you some dark secret. His thoughts go to the gold watch on his wrist but then he fights to keep the watch out of his mind. He briefly focuses on a pawnbroker's shop which is next to a diner. Could he be a pawnbroker? You will never know, for in the next instant he breaks line-of-sight and disappears into the crowd. You spring forward to try to relocate him, but it is no use. Meanwhile, the crowd has long since lost interest in its arguments and fifty wide-eyed faces are staring at you. You decide to leave. After changing, you may:

Head into Audubon Park	Turn to **165**
Go to work	Turn to **341**
Buy a paper	Turn to **228**

10

You leave the airport and head for home. What a day! You slump into a chair in front of the TV and relax with a long, cold drink. You may add 6 *STAMINA* points for the rest. One thing disturbs you. Your boss, Jonah Whyte, will be livid when you turn up for work tomorrow. You will have to invent some pretty convincing excuses... The next morning you set off to work early. You decide to travel by subway to make sure you get to work on time. But since when has a superhero's life ever been easy? 'HELP!' shouts a voice further up the crowded carriage. *'Pickpocket!'* Oh, no ... just what you needed. You force your way through the crowd on the busy train. As you reach the pickpocket's victim, that familiar *beep – beep – beep* sounds from your Crimewatch. Its electronic voice speaks: *'RADD SQUARE, HURRY.'* You sigh. But what will you do? The train is pulling into a station and you will have to change trains immediately if you are to reach Radd Square quickly. If you want to do this, turn to **201**. If you want to apprehend the pickpocket, turn to **185**.

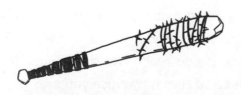

11

You fly up in the air to the floating vapour. As you approach it, you spin your body round in the air like a top. Your plan is working! You are sucking the brown cloud back down to the ground. As it swirls about, it begins to solidify and when you reach the ground, it has turned into the dazed personage of the Smoke. Although you have managed to defeat the arch-criminal – and you may award yourself 2 Hero Points for this – you have not managed to prevent him sending radio photographs of the doctor's notes to the headquarters of F.E.A.R. Turn to **162**.

12

Your Energy Bolt smashes into the side of beef speeding towards you, but hardly slows it down at all. Perhaps the freezing cold has affected your *Energy Blast*. But you have no time to wonder about this now. You must take evasive action. Turn to **436**.

13

You race down the escalator after him. But he has quite a head start on you; and he knows that you will not use your powers with so many people about. You start to gain on him as you reach the first floor. He looks over his shoulder and sees how close you are. You can tell he is beginning to panic. Halfway down the last escalator, he strips off his jacket and flings it at your feet. Suddenly you are falling forwards, your feet ensnared in the chains dangling from the jacket. Damn! As you land in a heap at the foot of the escalator, you see him disappear out of the door into the street. You will never catch him now. You pick up the jacket and search through the pockets for possible clues. Stuffed in one pocket you find a crumpled piece of paper and your eyes light up as you see the mark of F.E.A.R. at the top! The message reads: 'Don't forget. We need the merchandise in time for our meeting on the 28th. Do not fail us.' At least your effort has not been entirely in vain. You return to the third floor to make sure the other three thugs are handed over to the police. Turn to **380**.

14

You search his shop. The place is littered with cheap jewellery, cameras, electrical goods arid tatty furs. The back room is much the same. There seems to be nothing here. You may either leave and try the diner next door (turn to **351**), or try something else (turn to **368**).

15

Wisneyland is swarming with holiday-makers enjoying their day out at the amusement park. The smell of candy-floss and hot dogs hangs in the air and, as you stroll about, youngsters clutching stuffed animals run laughing past you. Screams of delight from roller-coaster riders turning through the corkscrew break through the general hubbub. You are going to enjoy yourself today. Which ride do you want to try:

The Big Dipper?	Turn to **187**
The Fun House?	Turn to **174**
The Dodgems?	Turn to **357**

16

You tie the three of them up and release Drew Swain, then summon the police on your Crimewatch. While you wait for them to arrive, you peruse the Mantrapper's fiendish traps. Apart from the bath trap which has made him famous (when the victim pulls the plug, the plug-hole opens up to swallow both him and the water), you are particularly impressed by a handkerchief net. When held by one corner and shaken, the handkerchief turns into a strong nylon net big enough and strong enough to trap a man. You run through the miscellaneous bric-à-brac which litters his work-bench and come up with what may provide useful information: you have found a diary. Reading through it, you learn that he has been in contact with Sidney Knox, a research assistant at the Murdock Nuclear Laboratories. Knox is a peaceful type who spends his spare time watching migratory birds from a tall observation tower at the Laboratory. But he is under the Mantrapper's control and will do his bidding. With this knowledge you may locate him easily should the need arise. If you are offered the opportunity to search for Knox, deduct 40 from the reference you are on at the time and turn to this new reference to locate him. You may add 1 *LUCK* point for this information. Eventually the police arrive and take charge. You may award yourself 3 Hero Points. Now turn to **428**.

17

You step back into the bushes to change, having decided it best to visit the jeweller's in your street clothes. You make your way to a seedy jeweller's you have seen on 9th Avenue. 'Nah. Cheap stuff,' says a crouched, balding man who rubs his unshaven chin. 'Don't get much call for monogrammed medallions. Tell ya what. Give ya five and a half for it.' You explain that it is not for sale and leave his store. Turn to **181**.

18

What a day! You slump into a chair in front of the TV and relax with a long, cold drink. You may add 6 *STAMINA* points for the rest. One thing disturbs you. Your boss, Jonah Whyte, will be livid when you turn up for work tomorrow. You will have to invent some pretty convincing excuses... The next morning you set off to work early. This time you will travel by subway to make sure you get to work on time. But since when has a superhero's life ever been easy? 'HELP!' shouts a voice further up the crowded carriage. *'Pickpocket!'* Oh, no... Just what you needed. You force your way through the crowd on the busy train. As you reach the pickpocket's victim, that familiar *beep – beep – beep* sounds from your Crimewatch. Its electronic voice speaks: *'COWFIELD DAIRY, FAST.'* Typical! Another dilemma! The train stops at a station only a block away from Cowfield Dairy. Will you leap out and see what is happening there (turn to **369**), or will you instead aid the pickpocket's victim (turn to **185**)?

19

The others are shocked at the defeat of their leader. They surrender to you. You lock them in their conference room and guide the jet back to Parker Airport where you hand them over to the authorities. Turn to **440**.

20

You spread the map out. It is a map of Titan City, and well used, by the looks of things. Fingers have rubbed the printing off one area and a small black cross marks the spot. It is approximately at the junction of 12th Street and 2nd Avenue. But there is no clue on the map as to what this could be. You fold the map up and put it back in your pocket. Turn to **86**.

21

The citizens of Titan City have turned out in their thousands to greet the President. They line both sides of 7th Avenue six deep, and the presidential car is still not due to arrive for half an hour. Spirits are high. There is much flag-waving and bands are playing in the streets as a prelude to the arrival. Will you spend the next half hour in a coffee bar waiting for the main procession to arrive (turn to **100**), or will you find a place in the crowd which offers a decent view (turn to **7**)?

22

At point-blank range, you fire an Energy Bolt into the Creature's chest. It howls in pain and releases its grip on the girders. It buries its head in its massive hands and you watch as a remarkable transformation takes place. The Creature writhes about and, as it does so, it shrinks in size! Before your eyes, it reduces to the form of a man and you recognize the face. The Creature of Carnage is none other than Illya Karpov, known agent of F.E.A.R. Karpov turns to face you and you must fight him:

ILLYA KARPOV   *SKILL 8*   *STAMINA 8*

If you defeat him, turn to **364**.

23

As the Silver Crusader, you step out towards the limousine. The police have cleared the crowd back to a safe distance. Two ambulances and a fire engine have arrived. The situation seems to be under control. But the spread of the fire is a little worrying: it is heading towards the tank! The two men inside the car – the chauffeur and his passenger – look thoroughly shaken. Will you use your super powers to aid the men (turn to **366**), or will you wait to see how the fire brigade do first (turn to **244**)?

24

You fling open the back door and your eyes scan the dirty yard outside. In the far corner of the walled yard is a pile of boxes and you can make out a shoe protruding from behind them. If you have *ETS* and wish to use a gadget, turn to **402**. If you wish to use *Psi-Powers,* turn to **209**. If you wish to use *Energy Blast,* turn to **344**. Otherwise turn to **232**.

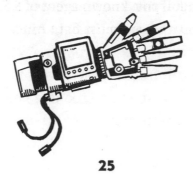

25

You stand powerless before him. He orders you to leave and you have no choice but to obey him. You step back towards the door, only to be startled by a loud *bang,* followed by the sound of shattering glass. The Poisoner slumps forward, a trickle of blood seeping from his forehead. The vial smashes safely on the floor. A face appears at the window and you breathe a sigh of relief. It is the office clerk, holding in his hand a smoking revolver! The danger is now over and you can leave the reservoir. Turn to **107**.

26

He takes you on a long trek through the zoo until you eventually reach the administration offices, where he introduces you to the Director. You ask him more about the escape. 'Good Lord, Crusader,' he says. 'I mean, yes, we have had an escape, but it's hardly a national disaster. After all, what harm can an escaping Aardvark do? Might eat a few termites, but I'm sure no one will shed any tears over that, will they?' An *Aardvark,* you think. The Director is right: it's hardly likely to cause any damage. You leave the zoo. Where will you go now? Do you want to follow up the call from the Egyptian Museum (turn to **158**), or do you think it will be too late now and instead head for home (turn to **113**)?

27

Like a sleeping giant, the huge pistons and cogs of the engine room are motionless. Suddenly, the squeak of a door opening startles you! Hiding behind one of the huge flywheels, you watch as a sailor enters, squirts some oil on a couple of wheels, and leaves. Routine maintenance. You climb the stairs back up from the engine room. Turn to **368**.

28

The Alchemist steps back and holds his tube up. Without warning, he dashes it on the floor and a pungent gas fills the bank. You fight to remain conscious, but to no avail. When you awaken, you are being shaken by a police officer. The Alchemists have disappeared, taking their booty with them. The cashiers and customers are likewise regaining consciousness, but two officers are kneeling over an elderly woman who does not stir. One of them looks up and shakes his head. She is dead! All eyes turn to you. Had it not been for your intrusion, the Alchemists would no doubt have simply run off with their money and no one would have been hurt. A cloud of despair descends over you. You are indirectly responsible for the woman's death! Your confidence is shaken and you must lose 1 *SKILL* point. Lose 2 *STAMINA* points as well, for the effects of the gas. Turn now to **372**.

29

Suspended in the mist, a small brown cloud is floating away from the house. If you have *Psi-Powers,* turn to **287**. If you have *Energy Blast,* turn to **203**. If you have *Super Strength,* turn to **11**. Otherwise turn to **153**.

30

What is the number of the building you are looking for on this avenue? Add the number to the number of the avenue and turn to this reference. If the result makes no sense, turn to **368**.

Roll one die and consult the table below to find out what damage the dog does:

1,2 or 3   The dog cuts you with its claw. Lose 2 *STAMINA* points.

4 or 5   The dog knocks you backwards into the wall. Lose 2 *STAMINA* points. It also breaks free and bites one of the bystanders (deduct 1 Hero Point in this episode).

6   The dog bites you. *Test your Luck.* If you are Lucky, you suffer 3 *STAMINA* points of damage, but survive. If you are Unlucky, this wound is fatal.

Now return to the previous reference. Each time a dog wounds you, you must return here to discover what the effects of the wound are.

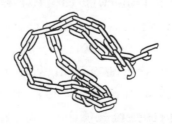

32

The Macro Brain's chopper detects your approach and turns to face you. You circle high and descend on the helicopter. You pick up speed. Five metres from your target, you hear the voice of the Macro Brain yell, *'FIRE!'* A wall of flame spurts from the front of the chopper! You are caught. You scream in agony as the flame burns you and you lose consciousness. Down and down you plummet, but mercifully you will never feel the impact as you crash to the ground...

33

You rush forward and crash heavily into the mutant, bringing him down to the ground. Resolve your combat:

SIDNEY KNOX   *SKILL 7*   *STAMINA 6*

If you defeat him, turn to **140**.

34

You arrive at the home of Dr Charles Crayfish, a well-known space scientist, on the outskirts of town. The rain seems to be coming down heavier here, and a mist is rising. The door is opened by the doctor's maid. She is surprised to see you. 'Oooh, the Silver Crusader!' she titters. 'Well, this *is* an honour! We do get lots of important people visiting – Dr Crayfish is working on the "Star Wars" satellite, you know – but we've never had a superhero come before. Do come in!' She tells you that the doctor is asleep at the moment; he was working very late last night. Do you want her to wake him up for you (turn to **66**), will you ask if you can have a look around his study (turn to **403**), or will you wait for him to wake and keep an eye on things in the meantime (turn to **257**)?

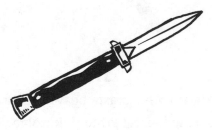

35

You hand the Tormentor over to the authorities and he is bundled off into a waiting police car. You stoop to pick up a piece of paper which seems to have fallen from his pocket. Opening it up, you find it appears to be a note scribbled down, perhaps from a telephone conversation. The note is ripped in half. Underlined at the top of the paper is FEA...' Under this is a message which reads: 'Meeting on 27th this mon...' You consider this for a moment, fold the paper up and tuck it into your belt. You may add 2 Hero Points. Turn to **10**.

36

You change and return to question the officer who immediately snaps to attention when he recognizes you. 'The Silver Crusader! Er, nice day ... I ... I mean no... Not a very nice day here. Awful. Ah, anything I can do to help?' You tell him to calm down and ask what happened. Apparently there has been a mugging. A wealthy businessman strolling through the park on his way to work had his throat slashed. But the officer knows no more. Presumably the police now have matters under control. There is nothing more you can do. Turn to **73**.

37

You take the key outside the room and find Grant Morley. But he shakes his head, telling you it is not his key. You leave the Fun House puzzling over your find, but your questions are answered when you see a young boy crying by his bicycle outside. He has lost the key to the padlock. You hand it over to him. You may add 1 Hero Point for helping him. Turn to **103**.

38

You visit the Grass as the Silver Crusader. He lives in a run-down part of town, in a dirty one-bedroomed apartment. He is horrified to see you, as your appearance will surely blow his cover. But, as always, he has some interesting information. Apparently, the Mantrapper has control of the mind of Sidney Knox, a research assistant at the Murdock Nuclear Laboratories. Normally a passive type – he spends all his spare time in an observation tower at the Lab watching migratory birds – Knox has been implanted with a post-hypnotic suggestion. No one knows exactly what this is, but Gerry's information will help you. If you find yourself looking for Sidney Knox, deduct 40 from the reference you are on at the time and turn to this new reference. You may add 1 *LUCK* point for this information. You leave discreetly and go home. The rest of the evening is uneventful and you may add 6 *STAMINA* points for the rest. Turn to **215**.

39

You head downtown towards the waterfront. But this is a large area to cover. Are you heading for the Oceanaria

Marina to check out the luxury yachts (turn to **370**), or for Clancey Bay, a navy dockyard (turn to **317**)?

40

The game has been abandoned and will be replayed at a later date. What will you do now? You may either go to watch the presidential cavalcade on 7th Avenue (turn to **21**), or you may go home to rest for the day (turn to **311**).

41

You rush into the bakery and ask questions about their last customer. But it seems there was nothing unusual about him. He bought a loaf of wholemeal bread and two custard tarts. The staff don't know anything more about him. If you have *Psi-Powers,* you attempt to read their minds (turn to **246**). If you have *Super Strength,* you may chase after the van (turn to **414**). Otherwise you may go outside to the scene of the crime and see if there are any other clues to be picked up (turn to **331**).

42

You look through the shelves for something unusual. What would he like? A biography? A thriller? You stop at a new section in the shop. Hmmm. Could be just right. 'Part game, part novel', eh? You buy him a copy of *The Warlock of Firetop Mountain.* Turn to **301**.

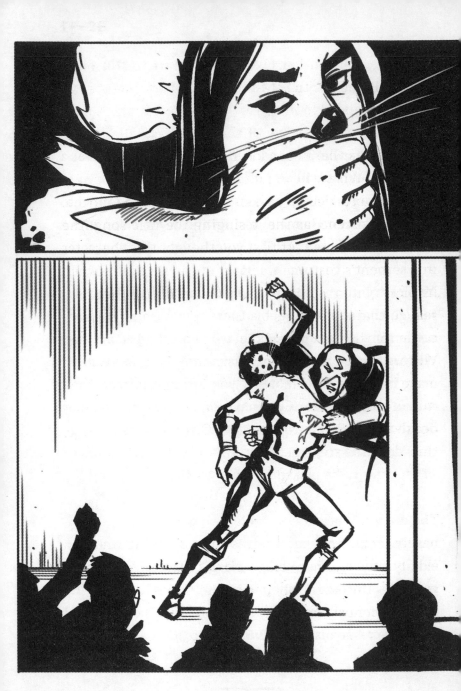

You realize that she has been kidnapped!

43

You are in luck. A ticket for tonight's performance has just been handed in. It is not the best seat in the house, but you get a good view of the show. It is all about a group of rats who live in a rubbish tip and sing to each other for amusement. A rather peculiar plot, you think, but you are particularly taken by the star, Lola Manche. In the last scene, as she is singing the title song, the show is interrupted. At first you thought this character in a serpent's costume was part of the show. But when he picks her up in mid-song and runs off the stage, you realize that she has been kidnapped! You find a dark corner in the back of the theatre and change costume. Will you wait outside the theatre for the kidnapper to make his escape (turn to **407**), or follow him backstage (turn to **169**)? You may remember your resolution and decide against intervening. If you will simply leave things be and go home, turn to **79**.

44

The dirty reception area confirms your suspicions. This hardly looks like the offices of a hi-tech exporter. An elderly lady with her hair in a bun raises an eyebrow as you enter the office. Will you rush past her to search the offices before she can stop you (turn to **199**), or will you see if she responds to a secret password (turn to **110**)?

45

You search around the cage for any signs of evidence that might relate the lions to the attack on the woman. You cannot find any. Eventually, you decide to give up this line of inquiry. Turn to **148**.

46

Only a single helicopter is inside the hangar. There are no ground crew around at all. The helicopter is a six-seater, perfect for a meeting. But you decide to hide behind a stack of crates in one corner of the hangar. In fact you are not expecting anything to happen for a couple of hours. What time of day are you expecting the meeting to take place? Add this time to today's date and add the result to this reference. If the resulting reference makes no sense, turn to **220**.

47

Turn to **34**.

48

The Bolt hits the creature square in the chest! It staggers a little, then turns towards you and roars. You try another, but the result is the same. Your Bolt has done no damage at all! The Devastator is composed of meteoric rock and cannot be harmed by your *Energy Blast*. It lunges at you with a great clubbed fist and knocks you flying across the room. Before you can recover, it has picked you up and flung you through the window. Luckily, you are still unconscious when you hit the ground, three storeys down...

49

You continue to try to reason with the man. While at first this seemed a hopeless exercise, you can tell that you are beginning to get through to him. Encouraged by the control-tower staff, you persist, persuading him that the only way he could succeed would mean his own death along with the lives of all on board. Finally he agrees to give up his mad scheme. He leaves the controls and unties the pilot, who then guides the plane down to safety. Turn to **285**.

50

You must now decide where you want to go. You may find what you are looking for at the junction with one of the streets. But which one? Add together the street and the avenue numbers and turn to that reference. If the result makes no sense, turn to **368**.

51

You call up 'Susan' and a young woman answers the phone. She bursts into tears when you tell her what is happening, and she agrees to come to the airport straight away. An hour later she arrives. Susan Blythe is young, attractive and distressed at what is happening. She agrees to talk to 'the Tormentor' over the radio. 'Richard!' she sobs. 'Richard, it's me, Susan!' There is a pause before a man's voice answers: 'Susan! What are you doing there?' 'Oh, Richard,' she answers. 'Don't do this! These people have done nothing to you! And I know that the girl was a private nurse now – but how was I to know at the time?' Gripping stuff, you think. But at least she's getting through to him. Ten minutes later, she has talked him out of his original plan. He agrees to land the plane safely, which he does, amid great cheers from the control-tower staff. If you have *Super Strength,* turn to **35**. Otherwise, turn to **285**.

52

You must react quickly. You have no time to concentrate on using your power. Turn to **436**.

53

With three of his buddies lying flat on the floor, the last Fire Warrior starts to get nervous. He shuts off his flames and races for the escalator. Do you want to pursue him through the store (turn to **13**), or do you want to make sure that the other three are handed over to the authorities (turn to **380**)?

54

An unmarked police car screeches to a halt by the barrier and two detectives climb out. Meanwhile you hunt through the bushes around the area. *Test your Luck.* If you are Lucky, turn to **405**. If you are Unlucky, turn to **91**.

55

You dive up into the air and zoom out over the water. The woman was right. Some thirty metres out from the beach, and advancing fast towards a young boy who is still in the water, is the ominous black fin of a ripper shark! You plunge down into the sea to take on the monster. Turn to **294**.

56

You circle the building for an hour, waiting for the Serpent to appear with his victim. One of the doormen comes running up to you excitedly. 'Round the back,' he pants, 'making off with Miss Manche!' You quickly nip round to the back of the theatre. But it is too late. The kidnapper has made good his escape and there is no sign of him anywhere. You have no choice but to leave the theatre and head home. Turn to **79**.

Twenty F.E.A.R choppers are headed towards the base

57

The assassin is about to take aim. You have one chance to use *Energy Blast* on him and, if you miss, you will have to leap on him quickly. If you hit, turn to **400**. If you miss, or if you would rather not use your *Energy Blast,* fight him hand to hand:

ASSASSIN   SKILL 9   STAMINA 8

If you win the hand-to-hand battle, turn to **258**.

58

You rush out into the drill square with the Colonel. He is barking orders at people around him and, through it all, a picture of what is happening emerges. Twenty F.E.A.R. choppers are heading towards the base, heavily armed. The soldiers are taking their positions. When the helicopters come into view you can see that this is a well-organized raid and you make a guess as to who has organized it. Amid heavy army fire, several of the choppers land within the perimeter fence. When a stocky man with a tall forehead in a black costume steps from the leading helicopter, your guess is confirmed. The Macro Brain! A product of genetic experimentation, like yourself, the Macro Brain has developed a tremendous intelligence. But unlike yourself, he has decided to use it to further the cause of evil. A formidable combination, you think. On your own there is little you could do against his well-disciplined private army. But if the Colonel's men could keep them at bay and you had the opportunity to face the Macro Brain on his own... As you consider this, a warning comes from your Crimewatch: *'COUNCIL BUILDINGS, FAST.'* You consider your options. If you wish to leave the army to cope with this struggle and will see what disaster is happening at the Council Buildings, turn to **154**. If instead you will try to get the Macro Brain on his own, turn to **208**.

59

You concentrate hard on the door mechanism, trying to will the door to open. But your situation is hopeless. The door is ten-centimetre solid metal and your thought-waves cannot get through. Some time later, more footsteps come down the corridor towards you. A startled face appears at the window. *'An intruder!'* cries the crewman. 'Locked in the ejection chamber!' You can guess what they will do next. A rumbling sound from the walls around you is followed by a loud hissing. Next thing you know you are forcibly fired out of the submarine into the sea. The shock is too much for you. You pass out, never to regain consciousness. It doesn't take long for your lungs to fill with water...

60

Just before you leave, you talk to one of the police officers who lives near Starkers Beach. There are reports of the sighting of a giant shark just off the beach and he would be grateful if you would investigate it. He has two children who swim every weekend and he is worried about their safety. You tell him you'll look into it. If you wish to go to the beach straight away, turn to **72**. If not, turn to **98**.

61

The sight of the transformation shocks you, and the Mummy advances. You are not sure how to tackle the creature. Will you rush in to attack (turn to **184**), or run back upstairs away from the creature (turn to **314**)?

62

The scene is one of mayhem. Injured people lie on the ground around the stand and others are panicking, trying to get away from the dangerous machine. If you have *ETS*, turn to **186**. If you have *Super Strength*, turn to **116**. If you have *Psi-Powers*, turn to **282**. If you have *Energy Blast*, turn to **304**.

63

You return home to change your trousers and nurse your leg. You may restore the lost *STAMINA* point. Then you set off again for work. Turn to **341**.

64

The man stutters nervously, 'The gun... He had a gun!' You hold out the water-pistol that you found in the kid's pocket and squirt him with it. His head bows. What a dreadful coward! He wishes to make amends. Yesterday two of his customers were talking and he overheard some information that may be of help. They both worked at Titan abattoir and reckoned that it had just been bought by a Sylvia Frost. When the shopkeeper heard the name, it stirred up a memory. He searched back through some old papers and discovered that Sylvia Frost was indeed the Ice Queen. This information may be useful to you. If you come across evidence of the Ice Queen's handiwork, deduce 20 from the reference you are on at the time and turn to this new reference. You thank the shopkeeper for his information and you may add 1 *LUCK* point for your good fortune. Now turn to **438**.

65

As your fist lands a mighty blow on its chest, something rather unexpected happens. The creature disappears! Along with the bystanders watching the fight, you stare in disbelief. Turn to **138**.

66

The doctor is not happy about being woken up and he barks angrily at the maid as he comes down the stairs in his dressing-gown. 'I don't care who it is,' he snaps. 'I am involved in very important work on the "Star Wars" satellite. I must have my rest.' You apologize for disturbing him and tell him of your fears that someone will be trying to steal his secrets. 'Nonsense!' he snorts. 'This house is wired up with a sophisticated alarm system. No one could possibly get inside without setting it off.' You explain that this may be no ordinary person and it would be wise for him to check his study. Turn to **303**.

67

You must start thinking about getting back to work. Outside it is starting to rain. Just your luck! Head for work by turning to **111**, if you don't know of anywhere else to go.

68

You search his shop. The place is littered with cheap jewellery, cameras, electrical goods and tatty furs. The back room is much the same. There seems to be nothing here. You may either leave and try the diner next door (turn to **351**), or try something else (turn to **368**).

69

The vial of phenolic acid breaks on the creature's chest and steam rises. The Devastator roars as it sees what is happening. The acid is eating away at its rocky chest! Clumsily, it tries to swat the steam away, but you can tell by its staggering movements that it is weakening. It falls to the ground beside the broken window and bellows mightily. Summoning up enough strength to pick itself up, it rises to its feet, sways and topples over sideways out of the window down to the ground below! You step over to the window. Three floors below it has shattered into fragments. The danger is over. Turn to **119**.

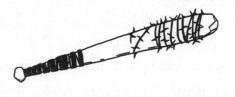

70

If you are staying in town, you will already be making your way towards F.E.A.R.'s secret meeting-place, which lies along one of the avenues. Which avenue are you heading for? Multiply its number by 10 and turn to that reference. If the result makes no sense, turn to **368**.

71

You leave the square to head for work. If only things were that easy. The Radd Square crowd has now focused its attention on you, and those papers and pencils are once more being thrust into your face. A weasel-faced man catches your eye: *'Pssst!* Hey, you, Crusader! Over here.' He looks a little suspicious and is holding a pencil and paper too. Will you go over and see what he has to say (turn to **126**), or will you do your public duty and sign autographs for the crowd (turn to **393**)?

72

Everything seems to be normal when you arrive at Starkers Beach. Hundreds of families are sunning themselves and splashing about in the water. Barely dressed girls are swaying in pairs along the walkway, tittering as they pass groups of muscle-bound gigolos, who try to attract their attention. Suddenly a single scream pierces the general hubbub. A woman's voice yells, 'SHARK! SHARK!' The reaction is immediate: the bathers panic and flee from the water towards the beach in a human wave. Your reaction is immediate too. What is your power:

ETS?	Turn to **299**
Energy Blast?	Turn to **180**
Psi-Power?	Turn to **146**
Super Strength?	Turn to **55**

73

You change back into your street clothes. Turn to **181**.

74

Getting the Prankster down from his secret chamber is no easy feat, but, with a carefully timed spring on the trampolines below, you manage to get back to the ground and can hand the villain over to police outside the Fun House. You may add 3 Hero Points for capturing the Prankster. Now turn to **103**.

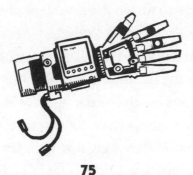

75

You remember that the President is coming to Titan City today. Do you want to go down to 7th Avenue to watch the presidential cavalcade? If so, turn to **21**. If you would rather not, you can go to watch your favourite football team, the Titan Tigers, play the Metro Mohawks instead (turn to **114**).

76

Your Aunt Florence is overjoyed to see you, but wonders why you are looking so untidy. She fusses about, making you tea and offering you cream cakes. You are exhausted by the day's activities and are happy to let her fuss. You decide to spend the night there, rather than face the long journey home. Next morning is, thank goodness, a Saturday. No work – if indeed you still have a job left to go back to at all! You leave your aunt's and you must now decide where you will go. There is an exhibition of 'Home Appliances of the Future' at the Whirl's Court Exhibition Centre. You may go there by turning to **425**. Or you may go to watch the presidential cavalcade on 7th Avenue; the President is coming to Titan City (turn to **21**). Alternatively, the Titan Tigers are playing a friendly football game against the Metro Mohawks. If you want to go and watch this, turn to **114**.

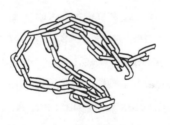

77

You are correct in your assumption. The freezing pool was no freak accident or malfunction of the heating equipment. It was caused by the Ice Queen, whose power of freezing touch has endangered the swimmers. You may track her down by turning to **129**, but first you had better return to **97** to rescue the two swimmers held by the frozen water.

78

You must fight the three of them, one at a time:

	SKILL	STAMINA
FOUR-ARMED BEAST	8	6
TIGER MAN	9	5
DR MACABRE	7	7

If you defeat them all, you may hand them over to the police. Award yourself 3 Hero Points and turn to **226**.

79

After a good night's sleep, you set off for work the next morning. To your great relief, your Crime-watch does not sound at all and you actually arrive before Jonah Whyte, who is astounded to find you hard at work when he arrives. You may add 2 *LUCK* points, as the danger of losing your job has now passed. At five o'clock, you leave. Will you change into the Silver Crusader and visit police headquarters to find out why so little has been happening on the crime front all day (turn to **245**), or will you pay a surprise visit on your aunt who lives out in the suburbs (turn to **134**)?

80

You draw a Mental Confuser from your Accessory Belt and try to turn it on. The mutant turns his attention towards you and concentrates. Your device will not work! Knox smiles as you fumble with the box and returns to concentrating on the reactor. You will have to fight him hand to hand. Turn to **33**.

81

Dropping your hands to your sides in a motion of apparent submission, you concentrate on the Poisoner. His hand moves to take the stopper off the vial of poison. He raises it up and starts to tip it. You concentrate harder and the villain screams! You are succeeding in forcing him to swallow his own poison! He pleads with you for mercy and you agree to will him to smash the vial *only* if he tells you what he knows about F.E.A.R. 'All right!' he stammers. 'I'll tell you this. Vladimir Utoshski is arranging a meeting soon. I am not invited. But I know this. The location of the meeting is known by a man with a gold watch.' With a last strain of mental effort, you will him to smash the vial on the floor. He does so and you step over to capture him. Turn to **227**.

82

You may take on the dogs one at a time (take on as many of the dogs as are in the crowd):

	SKILL	STAMINA
First RADIATION DOG	7	5
Second RADIATION DOG	6	5
Third RADIATION DOG	7	6
Fourth RADIATION DOG	7	7

The first time one of the dogs rolls a higher Attack Strength than your own, turn to **31**. But before you do so, *note this reference* as you will be instructed to return to it. If you manage to defeat all the dogs, turn to **193**.

83

You check the book records. Most of the boxes are listed as containing money, jewellery, old documents and computer data disks, and nearly all are held by wealthy citizens or local businesses. Most are in the main vault, which is now locked, but a number are scattered around the floor outside the vault door. One of these.contains some recently completed title deeds to Titan abattoir. They show that the abattoir has just been bought by a 'Sylvia Frost'. This name rings a bell. Sylvia Frost? Of course! The Ice Queen! If you find evidence of the Ice Queen's activities, you can use this information to locate her by deducting 20 from the reference you are on at the time and turning to this new reference. Now turn to **60**.

84

You rush out of the control tower and zoom up into the sky towards the low-flying aircraft circling the airport. You reach it easily and enter through the emergency door release. The rush of air alerts the passengers and they gasp as they see the Silver Crusader enter. You close the door and motion for everyone to remain calm. Luckily, the cockpit door is closed and the Tormentor has not noticed your entry. The way is clear for you to surprise the villain. You swing open the cockpit door. Inside, the two frightened pilots are tied against one wall. At the controls is a shaggy-haired madman whose wide grin turns to a look of astonishment as you appear. You must spring on him quickly:

THE TORMENTOR   *SKILL 8*   *STAMINA 9*

If you defeat him within ten combat rounds, turn to **346**. If you do not, turn to **376**.

The webbed claws of the grey-skinned beast flex as it steps towards y

85

The sky clouds over as you enter the cemetery and, by the time you are halfway across, the atmosphere is decidedly spooky. A scraping noise to your left attracts your attention. The noise is coming from a recently dug grave and you step over to get a closer look. Your eyes widen as you see a movement in the soil on the top of the grave. Something is trying to get out! A hand reaches out of the soil and you are frozen to the spot as a huge shape lifts itself out of the pit. You recognize the creature: you have come across him once before. The webbed claws of the grey-skinned beast flex as it steps towards you. The Reincarnation! The beast that cannot be killed! Why on earth has he been buried in an ordinary grave? Probably some idiot official didn't believe the stories. But one thing is certain. The Reincarnation must not be allowed to stalk Titan City again on its mission of destruction. If you have *ETS,* turn to **332**. If you have *Psi-Powers,* turn to **422**. If you have *Energy Blast,* turn to **352**. If you have *Super Strength,* turn to **373**.

86

The train stops at Grimm Street station and you get off to go to work. You try to settle into your desk discreetly. No such luck. 'Lafayette. Get in here *at once!*' No sooner had you stepped through the office door than Jonah Whyte's booming voice summoned you. You creep into his office, mumbling scanty excuses for being late yet again. 'Enough!' he yells. 'What do you think we are running here? A charity? Do you suppose I should be grateful that you even grace us with your presence? Very noble of you indeed to even bother coming in at all! Well, I tell you what. I'm feeling kind today. You can have the rest of the day off. *Without pay!* And if you're not in first thing tomorrow morning, you can start looking for another job!' You slink out of his office with your tail between your legs. How can you tell him what you've been doing? And now you've been suspended for a day. Where will you go? Will you spend the day at Wisneyland, the amusement park (turn to 15), or will you go downtown, perhaps to do some shopping (turn to 202)?

87

You streak out after the plane. As it is taking off, you catch up with it and force your way inside through one of the emergency entrance doors. Inside, the meeting has already begun in a special conference room which has been built into the plane. But your entrance has not gone unnoticed. As you step inside, the six delegates rise to their feet. All are overawed by your entry – all except one. 'Stand back,' growls a deep, electro-assisted voice. 'Our puny visitor is no match for the Titanium Cyborg.' The others watch as the huge, bald-headed shape steps forward. Part man, part robot, the creature has powerful electro-assisted arms, and a pulsing glow lights up in the goggles it uses for eyes. Do you have a Circuit Jammer? If so, turn to **411**. If not, you will have to fight the leader of F.E.A.R.:

THE TITANIUM CYBORG   *SKILL 18*   *STAMINA 20*

After the third round of combat, turn to **136**.

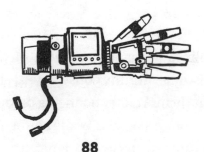

A notorious group of super-villains known as the Alchemists is planning a series of raids on financial institutions. The first victim will be the Cleveland Bank, at 4 a.m. Next will be another branch of the same bank situated on the corner of 128th Street and 10th Avenue.

89

You run down the hallway, looking for a fire-extinguisher. There is not one to be seen. Finally you find one in an empty room and bring it back into the lab. You break the seal and point it at the boiling bottle. Nothing happens! You check the instructions and realize that the extinguisher has not been serviced for two years! You try the next floor down and return with a functioning extinguisher. But as you arrive back in the lab, a wide smile has spread across Professor Murdock's face. 'Look!' he beams. 'The temperature is dropping! The danger is over.' The bottle has stopped its furious bubbling and seems to be cooling down. Relieved that the danger is past, you leave the building and head for home. Turn to **18**.

90

The trampolines are along one wall of the Fun House. They appear to be sturdily constructed; there is nothing special about them. You try bouncing on one and find that you can reach quite a height. While bouncing, though, you notice something suspicious. Higher up in the wall is a doorway, almost impossible to notice from the ground, as it is carefully blended into the wall. You bounce higher and find that you can reach a ledge if you bounce a little higher. Grabbing on to bars by the side of the doorway, you open the door and leap inside. Your hunch was correct. Standing at a control panel inside the room is a figure dressed in a red jester's outfit – the Scarlet Prankster, wanted for robbery and assault. You must apprehend this criminal:

SCARLET PRANKSTER   *SKILL 9*   *STAMINA 8*

If you defeat him, turn to **74**.

91

You find nothing in the bushes. You may as well leave this affair in the hands of the police. Turn to **73**.

92

Keeping a careful eye on the advancing lions, you reach in your Accessory Belt for your Aroma Emulator. You turn the controls to imitate the smell of catnip. The device hums and the lions stop in their tracks. They are anxious to get at the catnip. You fling your device to the back of the cage and the lions forget about you. Nor will they obey their keeper's instructions. The Ringmaster is appalled at how easily you have seen off the beasts and gives himself up to you. You take him back into the small room and go through his papers. One scrap of paper catches your attention – a message, written under the F.E.A.R. seal! The note reads: 'The password is *Quicksilver.* Memorize and destroy this message.' Now turn to **433**.

93

You take the murderer to police headquarters. On the way he pleads with you not to turn him in. He even gives you some useful information. Apparently the Serpent has been spurned by his actress girlfriend, Lola Manche. She is famous for her quote: 'I don't want to be a star; I just want to be an ordinary girl!' She always takes the poorest of dressing-rooms and has decided to give up her life of decadence as the Serpent's girl. He has sworn that, by hook or by crook, she will return to him.

Of course, you will not give way to deals with criminals. But you may add 1 *LUCK* point for this information. You hand Bronski over to a surprised sergeant at the desk and leave. You may add 1 Hero Point for your arrest. Turn to **67**.

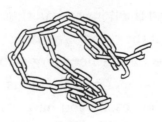

94

You need to do some shopping and you head for Schuter Mall, a couple of kilometres out of town. It is a huge site with hundreds of different shops. Do you want to go into the drug store (turn to **313**), the supermarket (turn to **160**) or the computer shop (turn to **264**)?

95

As you recoil from the wound, the shark frees itself from your grip and swims for the boy. It snaps its jaws around the youngster, whose cries turn to gurglings then to silence as a red cloud spreads through the water. You, and the onlookers on the beach, are horrified! The ripper shark flips its tail in the water, and disappears out to sea. You swim back to the shore and step out on to the beach with your head bowed. The crowds are silent, except for the sobs of the forlorn mother. The authorities can take over now. You quietly enter a cubicle and change clothes. When no one is watching, you leave the beach and head for home. Turn to **18**.

96

The enormous ship will take many hours to search properly. Nevertheless you must start somewhere. Will you start downstairs in the engine room (turn to **27**), or head for the captain's quarters (turn to **164**)?

97

You arrive at Stanley Pool and the doorman rushes you into the main hall where the pool is. Your jaw drops as you see the problem. The pool has frozen! Shivering swimmers are staring incredulously at the block of ice that, moments before, they were swimming in! Two girls, however, were not able to swim to the side in time and they are held fast in the ice, in danger of freezing to death. Their cries are getting weaker. You had better use your powers to help them quickly. If you have *Psi-Powers,* turn to **389**. If you have *Energy Blast,* turn to **307**. If you have *Super Strength,* turn to **338**. If you have *ETS,* turn to **231**.

98

As you leave the bank, you hear a bleeping coming from your wrist. Your Crimewatch is receiving a message from Gerry the Grass. The electronic voice speaks two words: *'PARKER AIRPORT.'* If you want to head straight away to the airport, turn to **410**. If, on the other hand, you have still not yet finished with the Alchemists, you may be heading somewhere else. If this is the case, deduct the avenue number from the street number and turn to this reference.

The tension is building as you shove your way into the centre of the crowd. The man and woman are screaming at each other, with the man threatening to strangle her dog if she does not clear up its mess. In the crowd the arguments are echoed. 'What would you think if *I* did that on your front doorstep?' yells a sweaty, bespectacled man. 'What do you expect the poor dog to do? The City Council should keep our sidewalks clean!' says a young student-type with his nose in the air. 'These days a dog's not safe on the road, even in the gutter!' pipes up another voice, and 'It's that fat frump who should be strangled, not the dog!' cries another. In the centre of the crowd, you find that you are not alone in trying to settle the tempers. Three others are trying to defuse the situation, without too much success. A jostling starts and you are kneed painfully in the thigh. You fall to the floor holding your leg. As if in response to your plight, the welcome sound of police whistles subdues the tempers and three black-shirted officers disperse the crowd. One of them picks you up from the ground and asks about your leg. It is painful, but not broken. Perhaps worst of all, though, was your unfortunate fall. For you have fallen straight into the cause of the whole commotion! Lose 1 *STAMINA* point for your bruised leg. Do you now want to go home and change (turn to **63**), or will you talk to the police officers (turn to **305**)?

100

Manny's Coffee Shop has never been so busy. The excitement surrounding the President's arrival has brought all sorts of people to the streets. You sit down at a table next to a man wearing a shabby brown overcoat and the two of you are soon talking. The man is very drunk and says more than he should. It seems he has connections with the underworld and lets slip some information. Apparently the Ocean Behemoth has been seen in Titan harbour and the man knows the purpose of the huge fish-creature's visit. It seeks revenge on the one who defeated it a year ago. That person was none other than yourself! You remember the encounter well. It is a huge water-spawned creature which cannot be allowed to enter Titan City. You make a mental note to explore the harbour as soon as you can. Now turn to **157**.

101

There is nothing around, except a garbage can by the back door. You pick up the lid and hold it in front of you as you step up to the door. Turn to **24**.

102

As you arrive downstairs, the police are forcing the crowd back away from the wreckage. To your horror, you can see the driver of the car and his passenger in the back seat, struggling with the doors. The fire is spreading and they cannot get out! Will you step round the corner and change into the Silver Crusader (turn to **23**), or will you wait to see whether the police have the situation under control (turn to **229**)?

103

Where are you heading as you leave Wisneyland? Will you make your way downtown to do some shopping (turn to **202**), or go home. If you decide to go home, you may either want to rest for the evening, in which case you may gain 6 *STAMINA* points (turn to **327**), or you may wish to sacrifice *STAMINA* gain and spend the evening at the theatre if you can get a ticket for tonight's performance of 'Rats' (turn to **43**).

104

You step, as the Silver Crusader, towards the scene. A police officer spots you and helps you through the crowd, which parts as you are recognized. On the ground in the centre of the crowd is the body of a man – a man of some means, by the looks of his expensive clothing. Lying next to him is a gold-trimmed briefcase. While the police busy themselves with moving the crowd on, you may choose to examine either the body (turn to **318**), the briefcase (turn to **211**) or the surrounding bushes (turn to **54**).

105

You concentrate hard from outside the door and *will* the dogs into submission. Their frantic barking dies down as your power reaches them. When all seems to be calm, you open the door and step inside. *Test your Luck.* If you are Lucky, turn to **401**. If you are Unlucky, turn to **213**.

106

You chase the pickpocket and seem to be gaining a little. The doors of the train start to close as it prepares to pull out of the station. The pickpocket seizes his chance and leaps through the closing doors in the nick of time. He has evaded you! Without revealing yourself as the Silver Crusader, there is nothing you can do. Turn to **86**.

107

The matter of the F.E.A.R. meeting is playing on your mind. Perhaps it would be useful to talk to Colonel Saunders who commands the army base out of town. The Colonel may have some news on the meeting; or at least you could compare notes. Will you go to the army base (turn to **342**), or will you follow up the earlier summons by your Crimewatch to Stanley Pool (turn to **97**)?

108

There is a new menace in town, as Daddy Rich's lawyers have just got him off a murder charge. He is an eccentric millionaire who has everything money could buy. He now gets his kicks by murdering innocent victims and revels in their fear. He has very expensive tastes and lives in a penthouse apartment at 113, 58th Street.

109

For all your strength, you will not be able to defeat the Mummy. Instead, when you have reduced it to 4 *STAMINA* points, you may use your strength to hurl it into an open crate and seal the lid. You may capture it, but not kill it. Resolve your battle:

MUMMY   *SKILL 10*   *STAMINA 10*

If you manage to trap the creature, turn to **2**.

110

You lean towards her meaningfully and whisper your password. 'Eh?' she asks, puzzled. 'What did you say? Speak up!' You try again. This time she looks at you as if you were some sort of crank. Her eyes pass up and down you and she frowns. 'Are you a crazy? Be off with you, or I'll call the police!' You decide that she probably will call the police and decide to take a quick look round the place first. Turn to **199**.

111

You change back into street clothes and get a move on. You are late for work again! You turn the corner on to Clark Street and stop as you pass Harrold's Department Store. A thought has crossed your mind: you could stop and buy your boss a present of some kind to apologize for being late. But then this would make you even later. Is it worth it? If you wish to go in and look for a suitable gift, turn to **429**. If you want to get to work as quickly as possible, turn to **301**.

112

The police and bank officials fall silent as you step through the door of the bank. Do you wish to interrogate the Branch Manager of the bank (turn to **420**), the Chief Detective investigating the case (turn to **323**) or the security guard (turn to **259**)?

113

On the way home, you notice a figure following you. Intrigued, you allow him to follow until you reach a corner, then you step quickly into a doorway and wait. Sure enough, the man appears, turns the corner and stops, scratching his head. You spring out and grab him. You demand to know why he is following you. He is quivering with fear and tells you that his boss, Fats Bluebottle, a well-known underworld figure, sent him to report on your movements. In his fear he also tells you some useful information. Apparently, one of Vladimir Utoshski's agents of F.E.A.R. will be at the forthcoming 'Home Appliances of the Future' exhibition. You may add 1 *LUCK* point for this information. You release the man, telling him to let Fats know that *you* will be watching *him* from now on, and the terrified spy scampers off away from you. Thinking about what he has told you, you head home, where you relax for the evening in front of the TV. Add 6 *STAMINA* points for the rest and turn to **215**.

Standing between two iron girders is a huge, hulking creature

114

You arrive at the stadium and buy your ticket for the game. It promises to be an exciting game, as both teams are evenly matched. You are hoping that the Tigers will have the edge: they recently spent over a million on fullback 'Streak' Gordon and you are anxious to see how he turns out. But neither side is able to maintain the advantage and by half-time a last-minute push by the Mohawks has levelled the score. The second half starts with a fabulous scoring run by 'Streak' Gordon. But, amid the excitement, screams of terror are coming from the crowd. Part of the stand is collapsing! You rush off to change and then nip underneath the stand to find out what is happening. You are amazed by what you see.

The collapse is not a structural fault, as you thought. Standing between two iron girders is a huge, hulking creature with brown, scaly skin, which is shaking the girders and groaning with the effort. You order it to stop. It sees your shimmering uniform and roars loudly: 'PUNY HUMAN!' it speaks. 'WHAT CAN YOUR PITIFUL EFFORTS HOPE TO ACHIEVE AGAINST THE CREATURE OF CARNAGE? MANY MUST DIE BEFORE I WILL BE STILL.' Again the creature shakes the stand and this time a crack appears in the metre-thick concrete above. You had better react quickly. If you have *Super Strength,* turn to **315**. If you have *Psi-Powers,* turn to **384**. If you have *Energy Blast,* turn to **22**. If you have *ETS,* turn to **163**.

115

You find a pair of overalls and mix with the cargo crew unloading the three aircraft inside the hangar. There is nothing suspicious about the crew or the cargo, but you expected this. In fact you are not expecting anything to happen for a couple of hours. What time of day are you expecting the meeting to take place? Add this time to today's date and add the result to this reference. If the resulting reference makes no sense, turn to **220**.

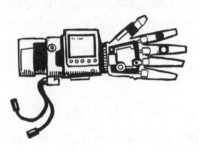

116

You fly into the air over the Android, grab it and hoist it up out of harm's way into the roof of the building. Finding a clear spot, you release it. It crashes down to the ground and fizzles, its broken limbs twitching harmlessly. You search for Vladimir Utoshski from your vantage point, but can see no sign of him and return to the stand. No one is now manning the stand, and you start rummaging through Utoshski's papers to see if you can find any clues. Only one piece of paper looks interesting; it is from the Parker Airport Authority, advising him that his booking requirements have been made. You also find a small pen-like gadget in a box labelled 'Circuit Jammer'. You decide it could be quite useful and take it with you. Add 4 Hero Points for defeating the Android. Your job done here, you leave Whirl's Court. Turn to **75**.

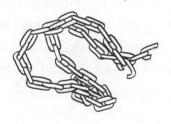

117

The dressing-room shows obvious signs of a struggle having taken place recently. Theatrical clothes, ripped and soiled, lie strewn about the place among smashed bottles of theatrical make-up. Evidently the kidnapper and his victim had something of a fight here. But where are they now? The open window gives the game away. It leads out into the parking-lot behind the theatre and, as you poke your head out to look for the Serpent, you hear the sound of squealing tyres. The Serpent has escaped with his victim! You will never catch him now. You change back into your street clothes and make for home. Turn to **79**.

118

Your information was correct. As you arrive at the junction, sounds of a commotion are coming from the bank. There are no signs of police. You look through the glass door. Two men in white lab coats are rummaging through the cashiers' drawers and stuffing notes in sacks. Another is grasping a test-tube rack containing five tubes of liquid and is holding another in the air ready to throw it at the cashiers and customers, who are huddled in a corner. All three are wearing rubber masks which make them look like ageing professors. *The Alchemists!* No doubt the test-tubes contain some of their dastardly creations. Will you burst through the door and leap on the one with the chemicals (turn to **437**), or will you wait to nab them as they leave the bank (turn to **309**)?

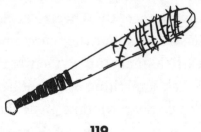

119

You are greeted by heroic applause from the crowd as you step from the library. The struggle has been a tough one, but you have defeated the strange creature. You may award yourself 5 Hero Points for the victory. Then turn to **319**.

120

Fight however many dogs are left, one at a time:

	SKILL	STAMINA
First RADIATION DOG	7	5
Second RADIATION DOG	6	5
Third RADIATION DOG	7	6
Fourth RADIATION DOG	7	7

Each time you are successfully attacked by a Radiation Dog, roll one die. If the result is a:

1,2 or 3   The dog cuts you with its claw. Lose 2 *STAMINA* points.

4 or 5   The dog knocks you back into the wall. Lose 2 *STAMINA* points and deduct 1 from your Attack Strength next round.

6   The dog bites you. *Test your Luck*. If you are Lucky, you suffer 3 *STAMINA* points of damage, but survive. If you are Unlucky, the wound is fatal.

If you defeat the dogs, turn to **350**.

121

Following the advice you were given, you change into the Silver Crusader and climb the fire-escape on to the roof of the Regent Hotel. You arrive just as the President's car is about to pass in the street below. Sure enough, in the far corner, a man is squatting. He is leaning over the edge of the roof and adjusting the telescopic sight of a high-powered rifle! If you have *Super Strength,* turn to **236**. If you have *Energy Blast,* turn to **57**. If you have *Psi-Powers,* turn to **177**. If you have *ETS,* turn to **194**.

122

Crowds of disappointed fans are milling around Addison Square Gardens. Tonight's concert has been cancelled: Georgie Boy is suffering from dermatitis. You decide instead to go home and rest. You may add 6 *STAMINA* points for the evening's rest. Next morning you do not have to go to work. Will you go instead to 7th Avenue to watch the arrival of the President, who is paying a visit to Titan City (turn to **21**), or would you rather go to Whirl's Court, where a special exhibition of 'Home Appliances of the Future' is opening (turn to **425**)?

123

A direct hit! Your blast strikes the ripper shark in the middle of its back, causing a gruesome explosion. Bits of shark meat and entrails fly high up in the air and rain down on the beach. The onlookers are revolted. Many of them are spattered with the creature's remains. Disgusted faces turn towards you. 'Trust that Crusader idiot to create such a mess. Ugh! It's nauseating! What was wrong with diving in and fighting the poor shark? Dumb animal – it didn't know any better...' Your jaw drops. What's wrong with these people? You've just saved a boy from almost certain death! With your head bowed, you leave the beach to change into your street clothes and head for home. Turn to **18**.

124

You hand the Tiger Cat in at police headquarters. You may add 2 Hero Points for this arrest. The police sergeant at the desk is puzzling over a piece of paper which has been handed in by a little old lady. She thinks it might be important. He lets you have a look at it, thinking it might be a clue. It reads: 'Watch for the sign of the Mantrapper – a metal slug with a letter M engraved on it.' This is a useful clue and you may add 1 *LUCK* point for seeing it. If you find evidence of the Mantrapper's activities, add 60 to the reference you are on at the time and turn to this new reference. Turn now to **67**.

125

You leave the Murdock Laboratories and head back into town. Walking along Danvers Street, you see a crowd huddled round a shop window and you step up to see what is going on. It is an electrical shop and the people are staring at a television in the centre of the window. A newsflash message is being reported by the announcer. You cannot hear what is being said, but you recognize the face on the photograph which appears briefly on the screen. It is Giorgio Schultz, better known as the Poisoner. What, you wonder, is he up to? Perhaps you'd better go down to police headquarters and find out. You turn to leave, and groan as a *beep – beep – beep* sounds on your wrist. Just what you needed! You lift it to your ear and listen to its message: '*STANLEY SWIMMING POOL.*' Where will you go now? To police headquarters (turn to **412**), or to the Stanley Swimming Pool (turn to **97**)?

126

The man draws you down an alley. 'Crusader, baby. Hi! Look, my name's Rat-face Flanagan. I ain't got much time to talk. Gotta get going. Here, read this. See ya. . .' You take the note he thrusts into your hand and read the message: 'There will be an assassination attempt on the President during his visit to Titan City. A decoy will be planted in the crowd. The real killer will be on the roof of the Regent Hotel.' This is an important lead and you may add 1 *LUCK* point for finding it. When the President is due to arrive, add 100 to the reference you are on at the time and turn to this new reference to apprehend the killer. Looks as though Rat-face is trying to get even with someone. Now you had better be on your way to work. Turn to **435**.

127

The Scarlet Prankster, a fun-loving criminal who delights in playing practical jokes on his unsuspecting victims, has found a new home and one most befitting his sense of humour. When you are in the vicinity of his new residence and are given the opportunity to look for him, subtract 50 from the reference you are on at the time and turn to this new reference to find him.

128

The gang has not noticed and you manage to shoo the boy and his mother away. If you have *Super Strength,* turn to **172**. If you have *ETS,* turn to **210**. If you have *Energy Blast,* you may not use it as there are too many passers-by. If you do not have *Super Strength* or *ETS,* turn to **243**.

'So! The Silver Crusader has come to pay a visit!'

129

You follow your clue's instructions to a seedy industrial area of town and arrive at the Titan abattoir. What sort of a place is that for a super-villain like the Ice Queen? The answer dawns on you as you pass a door leading to the refrigeration plant. Cautiously you open the door and step into the freezer room. Your breath freezes and you feel the cold at the back of your throat as you search through the sides of beef hanging in the room. A sound from behind you startles you. 'So!' speaks a woman's voice. 'The Silver Crusader has come to pay a visit! I hardly think you have come to stock up your freezer. I am honoured. Accept *this* as a gift!' You wheel round to see the sleek silver costume of the Ice Queen. Her long platinum-blonde hair partly covers her face as she shoves a side of beef towards you along a runner. If you have *Super Strength,* turn to **436**. If you have *ETS,* turn to **182**. If you have *Psi-Powers,* turn to **52**. If you have *Energy Blast,* turn to **12**.

130

His ears prick up as you whisper the word. You repeat it. He motions you to follow him and leads you into a steamy room at the back of the laundry. Underneath the sink is a trapdoor. He opens it for you and you climb down into a small space under the building. A single door leads from the chamber you stand in. Voices are coming from the door and a shaft of light runs across the bottom edge. Turn to **298**.

131

As the police arrive to help you with the bulky creature, a remarkable transformation takes place. The Creature of Carnage shimmers and shrinks slowly in size. Moments later it lies on the ground not as a creature at all, but as a man whose face you recognize. The Creature of Carnage is none other than Illya Karpov, agent of F.E.A.R.! You may add 5 Hero Points for this important capture; then turn to **40**.

132

The number you rolled is the number of Radiation Dogs that have escaped through the door and are now rushing into the screaming crowd, jaws wide open and frothing. You slam the door shut. Your immediate duty is to prevent anyone from being bitten! Your super power will be of no help here. Turn to **82** to fight the dogs. Fight only as many as escaped. If fewer than four escaped, return to **120** (note this reference), if you defeat them, to face the dogs left inside the Lab.

133

You jump over the counter and change quickly into the Silver Crusader. You will have to be careful not to stay too close to the Fire Warriors, as their flames will burn you. Perhaps just your presence will be enough to frighten them away. You spring out and order them to stop their foolishness and leave the store. They merely laugh at you. That didn't work. There is only one thing left for it. You will have to fight them:

	SKILL	STAMINA
First FIRE WARRIOR	7	6
Second FIRE WARRIOR	6	6
Third FIRE WARRIOR	7	5
Fourth FIRE WARRIOR	7	5

Fight them one at a time. Each time you are hit, roll one die. A roll of 1 or 2 indicates that you have been burned and must deduct an extra *STAMINA* point. If you defeat them all, turn to **380**.

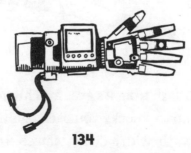

134

Your aunt lives in Cockney Green, a pleasant suburban district to the east of the Titan Centre. The bus drops you off at Cockney Cemetery, leaving you with a five-minute walk to her house. Will you take a leisurely stroll around the outside of the cemetery (turn to **219**), or will you take a short cut through it (turn to **85**)?

135

Two doormen are outside the curator's room. 'Ah, Abdul Aziz and Mustapha Kareem. Would one of you take our honoured guest on a tour of the exhibits?' They both stand to attention. 'Abdul, perhaps you would be so kind?' The man bows slightly and begins to escort you round the museum. There are many fine treasures in the building and Abdul Aziz gives you an interesting commentary on the life and times of the Pharaohs. The exhibits seem to be all intact. Finally you reach the largest room, which houses the exhibition's main attraction. Turn to **240**.

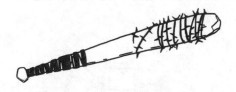

136

Bolts of light flash from its eyes and hit you square in the chest. The impact knocks you back against the wall. The Cyborg follows up with a deadly smash from its titanium-tipped fist. Your efforts are useless. The Cyborg is much too strong for you. Your last memory is its steely fingers tightening around your neck. . .

137

Grasping the door by its frame, you heave it off its

hinges. You grab both passengers and lift them away to safety. The man in the back, a middle-aged man in a fur-collared overcoat wearing an expensive-looking silver watch, is suffering from shock. He is delirious. As you lift him out of the car, he is mumbling incoherent bits of sentences: 'Fear summit... Must make meeting... Opposite number 35... Mustn't forget...' You hand him over to the ambulance-men to take care of him. And just in time, as the fire hits the tank and the car explodes. Your duty done, you may now nip off to change clothes and return to work. For your brave rescue, you may add 2 Hero Points. Turn to **398**.

138

An old man is attending to the girl in the water and another has gone to phone an ambulance. 'What is happening to the world?' he asks. 'Where does a creature like that come from? I have never seen anything like it before, except in my worst *dreams*. It's this new-fangled technology, I think. Creates super weapons in space and monsters on the earth. Bah! Sometimes I'm glad my time will soon be up. But Crusader, thank you for saving us. We all owe you our lives.' You can add 2 Hero Points for defeating the beast. You still don't know where it has come from, unless the old man has given you a clue. If you wish to try an address, add the street number to this reference to get there. Otherwise turn to **71**.

139

Daddy Rich pulls out a long-bladed silver knife and his two thugs do likewise. Fight his two bodyguards one at a time:

	SKILL	STAMINA
First BODYGUARD	8	9
Second BODYGUARD	7	8

If you defeat them, you may take on Daddy Rich himself:

DADDY RICH   SKILL 9   STAMINA 8

If you capture all three, you may turn them over to the authorities and award yourself 3 Hero Points. Then turn to **73**.

140

Knox lies unconscious on the ground and your attention turns to the reactor. Hissings are coming from the cooling pipes and one of them suddenly bursts, sending jets of superheated steam into a crowd of engineers.

Eventually, they get the leak under control, but the accident has cost the lives of four. You may add no Hero Points for this episode. However, the scientists are grateful to you for preventing what could have been a dreadful disaster. In appreciation of your saving the Laboratory, the scientists bring you a small pen-like device. 'Crusader, take this as a gift from us,' pleads the Institute Director. 'One of our men made this in his spare time. He calls it a "Circuit Jammer". It is still to be fully tested, but seems to work okay. I know you often face mechanical villains and their contraptions. With this, you will be able to disable their circuits. You are looking for Vladimir Utoshski and he is a powerful adversary. With this you will stand a better chance.' You thank the Director for his gift. It may well come in handy. Turn to **125**.

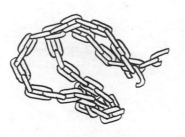

141

If this name means anything to you, you will have a seven-digit telephone number. Add all the seven digits together and turn to this reference.

142

You order Dr Macabre to give himself up. He is startled to see you and, as you aim your *Energy Blast* at his misshapen henchmen, he cries out: '*NO!* You cannot harm my creations!' He flings a bottle at you and it smashes against the wall. You aim a low-powered Bolt at the four-armed creature, who howls in pain as the Bolt strikes. Dr Macabre shrieks and holds his head in his hands. He gives himself up to you without a struggle. As you escort him and his miserable gang from the shop, you notice him quietly drop a small ball of paper on the floor. You pick it up and read it. Your eyes widen when you notice it is on F.E.A.R. notepaper. The message reads: 'Meeting changed to Clancey Bay.' After handing the mad doctor over to the police, you leave the Mall. Award yourself 3 Hero Points and turn to **226**.

143

Where do you want to begin your investigations? The Fun House's main attractions are buzzing with people, although most are now staring at you with open eyes. Will you check the 'Rotating Room' (turn to **439**), the trampolines (turn to **90**) or the 'Hall of Mirrors' (turn to **212**)?

144

You change into the Silver Crusader and head for the Biochemistry Department. There are no signs of panic; everything seems just like any other day. You make inquiries and find that a Professor Murdock is working on aldehyde experiments on the top floor. When you reach his Laboratory, the Professor is sweating profusely. 'Crusader!' he says, relieved to see you. 'My experiment has got out of hand! The temperature is building up! I fear I may have caused a disaster!' In the corner of the Lab, a complicated array of chemical equipment is shuddering. At one end a bottle is boiling madly. If you have *ETS,* turn to **295**. Otherwise turn to **339**.

145

How will you escape? You search in your Accessory Belt for something to use. You pull out your Laser-torch and begin to cut away at the door. The confined space makes you sweat, but your gadget seems to be doing its work. The metal on the door is ten centimetres thick and it will take some time before you can cut through. In fact it takes four hours... When you finally free yourself, you prepare yourself for action. Searching round the sub, which now seems to be deserted, you find signs of the meeting you were anticipating in a conference room, but no one is left. Despairingly, you leave the submarine and the dockyard. Turn to **368**.

146

You race down to the edge of the water and scan the surface. Your powers attract you towards one spot, which you search hard. Slicing through the surface, and advancing at an alarming rate towards a young boy who is still in the water, you can see the tall black fin of a ripper shark! You react quickly and concentrate all your energy on the water in front of the shark. The fin slows down. You are making the water more dense, so that the shark cannot swim as quickly. But there is one problem. The water around the boy is also affected and is preventing him from reaching the beach! You race over to the spot and dive into the water to take on the shark. Turn to **294**.

147

As you enter the pawnbroker's, the man behind the counter gasps. Before he can scream your name, you reach for him and clap your hand over his mouth to silence him. His fat face is sweating profusely and, as you grab him, he passes out. Something is certainly troubling the man! If you have *Super Strength,* turn to **68**. If you have *Psi-Powers,* turn to **188**. If you have another power, turn to **14**.

148

You change back into your street clothes and set off. A *beep – beep – beep* sounds comes from your wrist. As you hold your Crimewatch up, it speaks to you: *'MUSEUM OF EGYPTIAN HERITAGE.'* Do you want to follow its advice and head for the Egyptian Museum downtown (turn to **158**)? Alternatively, you are now not far from the home of Gerry the Grass. Would you prefer to pay him a call? If so, turn to **38**.

149

As you appear, a hushed silence spreads across the crowd. Your contemptuous look has its desired effect. They look at each other sheepishly and shuffle off along the sidewalk, going about their business. With the situation now well defused, you step up to the dog's mistress and reprimand her for allowing her dog to foul the footpath. Your duties as a citizen performed, you can now resume your alter ego and either set off again for work (turn to **341**), or go and buy a newspaper (turn to **228**).

150

You aim carefully and send your Bolt towards the vial of poison. It scores a direct hit! The Poisoner screams and drops the vial. You may now capture the injured villain easily. Turn to **227**.

151

You race down the street after the van. But by now it is long gone. Unless you have *Super Strength,* you are wasting your time. Turn to **428**. If you have *Super Strength,* turn to **414**.

152

A curious rumour is circulating through the more pleasant parts of the downtown area. It is rumoured that a young boy, known as the Brain Child, has extremely vivid dreams. In certain instances, these dreams seem to have come true. These are only rumours, but the identity of the child is known. He is Timothy Grant and lives on 100th Street.

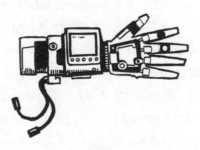

153

There is nothing you can do but watch the brown cloud float into the distance. The damage has been done. The Smoke, who has the ability to change into an ethereal form, has been through the doctor's notes and sent radio photographs to the headquarters of F.E.A.R. Turn now to **162**.

154

You speed off back to Titan City and arrive at the Council Buildings. Everyone seems surprised at your visit. The day has been a peaceful one. Being a holiday, there are few people about. There certainly seems to be no danger. Your Crimewatch beeps again: *'SORRY, FALSE ALARM.'* Just what you needed! Turn to **311**.

155

The noise from outside has made the Alchemists nervous. They tie up their sacks and race into the street to escape. Turn to **243**.

156

You jump over the counter and, while no one is looking, change into the Silver Crusader. You are well prepared for outbreaks of fire and you take the Micro Extinguisher from your Accessory Belt. Stepping up to the villains, you douse them with a blast of carbon dioxide and extinguish their flames. Coughing and spluttering, they give themselves up to you. Turn to **380**.

That crack sounded like a gunshot!

157

While you are trying to pry more information out of the man, you forget about the time. Suddenly the noise from the crowd outside swells up. The President is arriving! You leave the table and push your way out into the street. But before you can catch a glimpse of the procession, a loud *crack* sounds, followed by shouts and screams. You freeze. *Surely not!* That crack sounded like a gunshot! And from the reaction of the crowd, your fears could well have been realized. You nip inside a doorway and change into the Silver Crusader. When you fight your way through the crowds to the President's car, it is all over. He has been shot neatly through the chest and killed immediately. The bullet has been dug out of the car seat and you turn it over in your hand. Four letters are engraved in it: F-E-A-R. The outlawed organization has succeeded in assassinating the President! You *must* capture the heads of F.E.A.R. at their meeting before they are able to wreak any more havoc on the world. Turn to **311**.

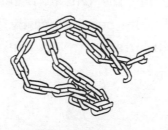

158

The Museum of Egyptian Heritage is in the mid-town area. Everything seems perfectly normal when you enter and you make for the Head Curator's office. Dr Kablah is an elderly professor-type with white hair and a thick white moustache that hangs over his mouth. He is surprised to see you but assures you that, as far as he knows, everything is in order. He offers to double-check all his treasures to make sure nothing has disappeared. Do you wish him to do this (turn to **416**), or will you ask him to get someone to show you round (turn to **135**)?

159

You press the button on your Circuit Jammer. The Cyborg's grin fades as the device affects its electronic functions. Its abilities have been reduced to those of an ordinary man! Now you may battle the creature on more equal terms:

TITANIUM CYBORG   *SKILL 9*   *STAMINA 10*

The others watching the fight are frightened to see their leader stripped of his power so easily. If you defeat the Cyborg, they will surrender to you. Turn to **440**, if you win this battle.

160

As you push your trolley around the shelves, you notice

a young boy stick a pack of Munchie Bars in his pocket and leave. Will you ignore the incident (turn to **424**), or apprehend the young thief (turn to **8**)?

161

The curator is mildly amused at your suggestion that his stuffed animals could have anything to do with the killings. 'I see,' he chuckles, with more than a little mockery in his tone. 'The elephant stepped off his pedestal and told his cleaners, "Excuse me, won't you. I'm just off out for a stroll round the grounds." And you think the tiger somehow passed right through its glass case, came downstairs – through the crowds, who didn't notice anything odd – left for a morning in Audubon Park and then returned at lunch-time? I thought you superhero-types were supposed to be bright. . .' You feel a bit foolish for even suggesting it. You decide to leave. Will you head for the zoo (turn to **408**), or try somewhere else (turn to **148**)?

162

You decide to return to town. You have already missed part of the day and Jonah Whyte will be furious when you return to work. Do you want to take the rest of the day off at Wisneyland, an amusement park you pass on the way into town (turn to **15**), or will you catch a bus back to work to make sure your attendance record doesn't get any worse (turn to **225**)?

163

You have nothing you can use against so powerful a creature. You will either have to take it on with your bare hands, or run off to fetch extra help. If you wish to get extra help, turn to **353**. Otherwise, resolve the battle:

CREATURE OF CARNAGE   *SKILL 12*   *STAMINA 14*

If you defeat it, turn to **131**.

164

The captain's quarters would be the obvious place for a high-level meeting. His rooms are immaculate, with a fine view out over the bay. But they are deserted: there is no one inside. You leave and return to the shore. Turn to **368**.

165

You arrive in the park to find a crowd dispersing and an ambulance pulling away. The police are getting back into their cars and driving off. A single car remains, with one police officer standing by a barrier which is marking out an area where the incident – whatever it was – must have taken place. A deep red stain marks the footpath behind the barrier. You talk to the officer. He is not interested in your inquiries, but you do manage to squeeze one word from his tight lips: 'Mugging.' Do you want to change into the Silver Crusader to persuade him to tell you more about what happened (turn to **36**), will you leave him and investigate the surrounding bushes (turn to **54**), or are you wasting your time here, since the crime has already been committed (turn to **181**)?

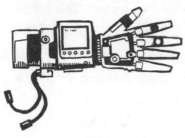

166

You gain ground and catch up with the pickpocket. As you grab him, he spins round to face you and draws out a knife! You will have to fight him with your bare hands, as you cannot risk revealing yourself as the Silver Crusader:

PICKPOCKET   *SKILL 7*   *STAMINA 6*

If you defeat him, turn to **296**.

167

You settle back down at your desk. On the corner of the desk is a newspaper open on page three. You flick through the pages and find a short piece which catches your attention. Your old enemy, the Smoke, is up to his tricks again. A known agent of F.E.A.R., the Smoke is able to turn into a gaseous form to commit his crimes. An incorrigible self-publicist, he cannot resist tantalizing the police with clues as to where he will next strike and often uses the newspapers to announce his intentions. If you can only crack his clue. He is quoted as saying, 'What sort of fish does not like the water? You'll find out when it next rains...' You will crack this clue by subtracting 20 from the reference you are on when you are told it is raining, and turning to this new reference. Turn now to **398**.

168

Although you may well have something in your Accessory Belt which you can use against the Tiger Cat, you have no time to use it. Resolve this combat:

TIGER CAT   *SKILL 9*   *STAMINA 8*

If you win, turn to **124**.

169

You rush across the stage and disappear into one of

the wings after the kidnapper. Stairs lead down to the dressing-rooms. At the foot of the stairs are three rooms. Room number one has two stars on the door. The door to room number two has one star and is slightly ajar. Room number three has no stars on it. Which will you try:

Room number one?	Turn to **322**
Room number two?	Turn to **288**
Room number three?	Turn to **250**

170

You may defeat the Mummy with *Energy Blast,* but you will have to use a much more powerful one than normal. When you first hit the Mummy, you will realize this, but not before. Therefore you must lose at least 4 *STAMINA* points in this battle. If you wish to escape, turn to **314**. If you defeat the Mummy, turn to **431**.

171

You arrive just in time. As you are about to enter the building, three men turn the corner towards you. In his gold and furs, Daddy Rich is returning home, flanked by his two burly bodyguards! They hesitate when they see you. Speckles of blood on his cuffs and shoes confirm your suspicions. If you have *Energy Blast,* turn to **371**. Otherwise, turn to **139** to confront Daddy Rich.

172

With your *Super Strength,* you pick up a heavy sidewalk sign outside the next-door store. As the Alchemists emerge, you fling it at them. A strike! The sign smashes into them, knocks two of them out and leaves the third so groggy that it is an easy matter for you to capture him. Turn to **336**.

173

'So!' laughs Dr Macabre. 'We are honoured to have the famous Silver Crusader witness our little shopping trip. Beware, my beauties. Guard your minds well.' You concentrate on Macabre himself and can gradually feel his will slipping as you take control of his mind. Eventually you feel you have captured his will and you order him to bring his creations out of the drug store. The three figures follow their master's orders and they walk towards you. But when they reach you, the two misshapen beast-men strike! Six arms grab you and fling you to the ground! You look up in time to see the Tiger Man's sharp jaws closing around your neck. You have failed in this struggle, and lost your life...

174

You pay the admission charge and enter the Fun House. You walk along a narrow passageway. As you turn a dark corner, a luminous skeleton appears in front of you, shrieking wildly! You jump, and then laugh; just one of the scares of the Fun House. Further down the passage, your feet stumble on a wobbly floor. Then the walls begin to sway. Suddenly, your foot steps on something and you fall forwards. But this time it is not a wobbly floor; you fall through the ground and land on a rubber mattress in a dark pit. Although it is pitch-black, you can tell that you are not alone. Another figure touches you! A voice calls but and you answer. 'Oh, thank God someone else is here!' gasps a man's voice. 'I have been here for two hours! I can't find a way out. And not only that, my wallet has gone. I'm sure it has been stolen. And I don't think this was any accident. My name is Grant Morley, a reporter on the *Titan Times*. I have been covering an exposé to reveal the identity of the Scarlet Prankster. Earlier I met an informant at the Big Wheel who gave me a key to one of the rooms here where he thought I could get some useful information. That key was in my wallet!' You consider the situation. The Scarlet Prankster is a dangerous criminal who delights in grisly practical jokes. You decide to change into the Silver Crusader under cover of the pitch-blackness. Then the two of you search the walls for a way out. You find a hidden door which lets you into the main room of the Fun House. If you have *Super Strength,* turn to **248**. If you have *ETS,* turn to **271**. If you have *Psi-Powers* or *Energy Blast,* turn to **143**.

175

You remember your clue. You ask someone about such a room and you are directed to the observation tower. Hoping that this may lead you to the mutant, you rush up to the room at the very top. There, staring out of the window at the huge reactor structure, is a man in a white coat with a bloated head the size of a pumpkin! You creep up behind him, deliver a blow to the back of his neck to knock him out and carry him downstairs to the waiting scientists. You can only hope that they can find a way either of curing him or of taming his destructive urges. Though you do not realize it, you have saved perhaps the whole of Titan City from a deadly threat by capturing Sidney Knox. In appreciation of your saving the Laboratory, the scientists bring you a small pen-like device. 'Crusader, take this as a gift from us,' pleads the Institute Director. 'One of our men made this in his spare time. He calls it a "Circuit Jammer". It is still to be fully tested, but seems to work okay. I know you often face mechanical villains and their contraptions. With this, you will be able to disable their circuits. You are looking for Vladimir Utoshski and he is a powerful adversary. With this you will stand a better chance.' You thank the Director for his gift. It may well come in handy. You may award yourself 5 Hero Points for saving the plant. Turn to **125**.

176

There is only one thing you can do from the ground. You step up to the radio and try to convince the Tormentor of the folly of his ways. The madman gloats at your miserable pleas. But from the tone of his voice, you can tell that he is impressed. Roll two dice. If the total is *less than* your *SKILL,* turn to **49**. If the total is *equal to or greater than* your *SKILL,* turn to **260**.

177

You have no time to use your *Psi-Powers,* as the assassin is about to fire. You leap on him from behind and the two of you struggle on the roof:

ASSASSIN   SKILL 9   STAMINA 8

If you defeat him, turn to **258**.

178

You concentrate hard, trying to force droplets of water out of the air to extinguish the flames. But it is no use. One of them puts his hand on a counter of socks and flames begin to rise. You had better act quickly. Turn to **133**.

179

You find yourself at the foot of a three-storey building. A scruffy-looking Chinese laundry is open on the ground floor. By the front door are stairs which go up to the other floors. A nameplate by the stairs reads: 'Chomsky and Sons: Exporters in Biomechanical Engineering'. Will you go in the Chinese laundry (turn to **266**), or will you investigate Chomsky and Sons (turn to **44**)?

180

You rush to the edge of the water and scan the surface. Thirty metres out from the beach you find what you are looking for. The tell-tale black fin of a huge ripper shark is cutting its way towards the beach. Directly in its path is a young boy, and in seconds the shark will have reached him! You have one chance to use *Energy Blast* on the creature before it reaches the struggling boy. Roll two dice. If the number rolled is *less than or equal to* your *SKILL* score, turn to **123**. If the number you roll is *higher than* your *SKILL* score, turn to **255**.

181

The familiar bleeping on your wrist alerts you. Your Crimewatch is receiving a message. The electronic voice speaks two words: *'PARKER AIRPORT.'* Hurriedly you change into the Silver Crusader and speed towards the outskirts of the city. It never rains but it pours: halfway there, the Crimewatch bleeps again! This time the voice is warning you of another incident, at *'PETER LABORATORIES.'* You have no indication of which is more urgent. Where will you go? To Peter Laboratories (turn to **284**) or to Parker Airport (turn to **410**)?

You leap aside to avoid the frozen bulk speeding towards you. *Test your Luck.* If you are Lucky, you avoid it. If you are Unlucky, it smacks into you, doing 2 *STAMINA* points of damage. From your Accessory Belt you draw a Low-Powered Heat Laser and point it at the Ice Queen. You press the button and send a pencil beam of heat at your foe. She winces as it stings her and holds out her hand. A similar beam of ice turns into a frozen shield which forces the laser beam back towards you! The two powers struggle against each other, backwards and forwards, as if both energy sources were arm-wrestling. You worry about the Laser's power source, but then you see signs that she is weakening. Her icy shield falls back and eventually disappears, and she squeals in pain as the laser heat – which would be no more than mildly uncomfortable to an ordinary person – burns her. She pleads with you to stop and offers you some information which will be useful. You release the button. 'Keep it off!' she screams. 'I will tell you what I know about the F.E.A.R. meeting you are trying to locate. I don't know exactly where, but the meeting is certainly somewhere on 3rd Avenue!' With your device trained on her, you bind her hands and feet. Turn to **241**.

183

Warning the police and staff to hide behind cover, you release a ferocious blast at the vault. The metal smoulders and melts a little, but the door does not open. You breathe heavily and beads of sweat break out across your forehead. The blast was highly charged and you must lose 2 *STAMINA* points. You are not sure whether or not you have the power to break through the solid steel door. If you wish to try again, turn to **275**. If you don't want to risk losing any more *STAMINA,* turn to **60**.

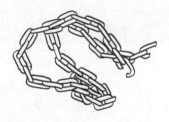

184

You land a fair blow on the creature. But rather than being knocked back, the Mummy's chest collapses under the blow and then re-forms. Your punch has done nothing! Staring in disbelief, you are off guard as the creature fastens its hands around your neck. Your struggles are futile, as its hands tighten their grip. This is the end of your career as the Silver Crusader. . .

'He ... he's stolen my wallet!'

185

You rush up to a puny-looking bespectacled man who is shaking with fright. 'There!' he cries, pointing to a man running up through the next carriage. 'He... he's stolen my wallet!' You race after him. No one else moves; they don't want to get involved. If only you could change into the Silver Crusader. Roll two dice and compare the total with your *SKILL* score. If the total is *less than or equal to* your *SKILL*, turn to **166**. If the total is *greater than* your *SKILL*, turn to **106**.

186

You quickly pull a Power Drainer from your Accessory Belt and attach it to the Android's back. You wait for its actions to slow down as your device begins to drain its internal batteries. But nothing happens! A light on the Power Drainer comes on. Its power supply has run down! You curse and think desperately about what else you could use. The answer comes from a man in the crowd who has been watching the demonstration. 'Try this,' he shouts, throwing you a small pen-like device. 'The demonstrator was asked what happens if the Android becomes uncontrollable and showed us this. He called it a "Circuit Jammer" or something. Maybe it will help.' You catch the device and hold it to the Android. Sure enough, the little gadget lives up to its name and the movements of the Android cease. The crowd calms down as the machine grinds to a halt, eventually toppling over to land harmlessly on the ground. This looks like a useful device and you keep it with you. You may also add 4 Hero Points for defeating the Android. Turn to **75**.

187

You climb into a carriage behind a couple with a young daughter. As you set off up the long climb, the excitement is mounting. Squeals come from the riders as the first steep drop lifts their stomachs. It is not until you reach the first sharp bend that you notice the danger. The young girl in the seat in front of you is wearing a safety harness which is hanging on by only a couple of threads! As you streak into the bend and are wrenched to the right, the harness snaps and the girl lurches across the carriage. Can you rescue her before she falls to her death? Roll two dice and compare the total with your *SKILL*. If the roll *exceeds* your *SKILL*, turn to **224**. Otherwise turn to **415**.

188

Just before the pawnbroker passed out, you managed to catch a strong mental image. He was obviously concerned about something, and a vision of a secret trapdoor flashed through his mind. You search the shop and indeed you find a trapdoor, hidden underneath the counter. You open it and step down into a small chamber. A door leads off from the chamber. Voices are coming from behind the door and a line of light comes from underneath it. Turn to **298**.

189

You find there is a new Michael Clackson album called 'Wilier', all about spooks and ghouls, and decide to buy it. You go straight home to listen to it. Turn to **327**.

190

You arrive at Central Hospital and ask at the desk about the strange admission. You are regarded suspiciously and one nurse, turning her nose up, says: 'Why do you want to know? Are you one of those gutter-press reporters?' You show her the emblem on the chest of your costume, but she is unimpressed. Finally, a police officer fills you in. 'Yeah, I know who you're looking for, Crusader. Something strange going on there if you ask me. But the guy died an hour ago. He's gone down to the morgue.' There's not much more you can do here. Will you leave and head for your aunt' s (turn to **134**), or do you want to check the morgue anyway (turn to **395**)?

191

In your shimmering costume, you step towards the crowd. If you have *ETS,* turn to **418**. If you have *Psi-Powers,* turn to **9**. Otherwise turn to **149**.

192

You concentrate on the creature's mind. Its head swings round to face you, as if it can sense your powers. But you can make no sense of the thought-waves reaching you. Certainly they are not of this earth. Will you take the creature on with your bare hands (turn to **262**), or will you decide that the army will stand a better chance than you and leave them to it (turn to **319**)?

193

If there are any dogs still left in the Lab, you must face them. Turn to **120**, but fight only as many dogs as are left. If you have defeated all the dogs, turn to **350**.

194

The assassin is taking aim. There is no time to use a device from your Accessory Belt. You will have to leap on him and grapple with him hand to hand:

ASSASSIN   *SKILL 9*   *STAMINA 8*

If you defeat him, turn to **258**.

195

A slim, red-haired woman opens the door and introduces herself as Wayne Bruce's wife. You break the news to her gently and, to your astonishment, she takes it unemotionally. 'There was nothing left between Wayne and me,' she says. 'I despise the man. I wouldn't wish him dead, but now he is, I couldn't give a damn. I certainly didn't kill him, if that's what you're thinking. And I've no idea who might have done. Maybe someone at the office will know. I don't.' If you have *Psi-Powers,* turn to **348**. Otherwise you may either try his office (turn to **233**), or leave the whole affair to the police (turn to **73**).

<h2 style="text-align:center">196</h2>

You circle the building, waiting for the villain to make his escape. Ten minutes later, a door opens and a serpent-headed man in a rough green costume steps out, holding Lola Manche in his arms. You stand before him and order him to drop the starlet. A wide grin spreads across his face and he hisses. He drops the girl obligingly and turns to fight you:

THE SERPENT   *SKILL 8*   *STAMINA 8*

The Serpent has a powerful secret weapon – his poisonous bite. Each time he hits you, roll one die. A roll of 1 or 2 indicates a bite and the poison will take effect. Deduct 1 *SKILL* point each time you are bitten. However, the effects of the bite are only temporary. You will recover your *SKILL* after one full day. If you defeat the villain, turn to **432**.

197

Having defeated the shark, you turn to the young boy, who is splashing about in the water, terrified. You calm him down, lift him out of the sea and carry him back to the beach, where his sobbing mother is waiting. She thanks you again and again and wants to know if she can do anything in return. Her uncle runs a circus and she could get you the best seats. You humour her and thank her for her generous offer, but insist that there is really no need. But your protests are of no avail. She writes down a telephone number, 444–5666, and tells you to ring a 'Captain Menagerie' any time you would like to see his show. She goes on and on about this uncle of hers. She tells you that he is the ringmaster of a circus and has strange habits. He has a secret office reached underneath the lion's cage where he keeps his money and papers. This information may be useful to you. If you ever need to find him, you may search for him by adding 50 to the reference you are on when you reach a lion's cage. By now this woman is becoming a pest. You excuse yourself. You really must be on your way. After secretly changing back into your street clothes, you head for home. Turn to **18**.

198

You fly up towards the central dome of the Fun House. Sure enough, your information was correct. High up the wall of the Fun House is a door. You alight outside the door, burst inside and startle a hunched figure dressed in a colourful jester's costume. He grabs for a piece of paper on the table in front of him and tries to stuff it into his mouth! But you are too quick for him. You manage to stop him eating the paper and must now fight him:

SCARLET PRANKSTER   SKILL 9   STAMINA 8

If you defeat him, turn to **333**.

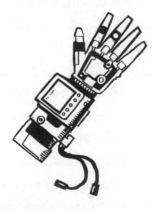

199

You search round the premises for signs of criminal activity. But all are deserted except one, in which a middle-aged man is asleep at his desk. He is naturally startled at your arrival and asks if he can help. Apparently business has not been good recently. There doesn't seem to be anything strange going on here. Turn to **368**.

200

Your Bolt misses and the Fire Warrior piles into you, fists swinging. You manage to fight him off, but not before he has given you some nasty burns. Lose 4 *STAMINA* points. While you are recovering, the four Fire Warriors make off down the escalator and out of the shop. The shop staff are putting out the fires that have been caused, and they look at you scornfully. 'I thought this Crusader character was supposed to be a hero,' sneers one. 'Pretty pathetic if you ask me.' You limp off downstairs and leave the shop. After finding a suitable place to change back into your street clothes, you head for work. Turn to **301**.

201

Radd Square is one of Titan's City's most pleasant areas. On a sunny day, the cool sprinkling of the fountain is refreshing and the blossoming cherry trees make it a picturesque place for the locals to eat their lunch and chat. The crowd you have noticed has gathered round the fountain. You change into the Silver Crusader and step over to see what is happening. As you arrive, you hear a piercing scream and panic suddenly hits the crowd. They turn and flee from the fountain. You rush forward to see what is happening. Rising out of the water is a huge figure, some four metres high. Its vast, bulky shape is green and scaly. It opens its huge jaws and leans forwards, snatching a fleeing woman and holding her high. You leap up to fight the creature. If you have *Super Strength,* turn to **272**. If you have *Psi-Powers,* turn to **326**. If you have *Energy Blast,* turn to **367**. If you have *ETS,* turn to **404**.

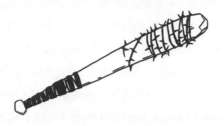

202

Strolling downtown, you stop first at the bank to get some cash. Next stop is a pizza parlour for a bite to eat. You take a stool facing out across Banner Street and watch the shoppers passing as you eat your pizza. On the far side of the road is a man you recognize. It is Drew Swain, a retired millionaire who made his fortune manufacturing the collection tins used by charities. He steps into a baker's shop; when he comes out, something strange happens. He takes a step forward and suddenly freezes, held like a statue in an off-balance pose. A blue van draws up and obscures your view. When the van drives off, Swain is gone! You saw it with your own eyes! But it happened so quickly that you are now a long way behind the kidnappers. Will you nip to the toilets in the back of the shop and change costume? If so, will you follow the van (turn to **151**), or ask questions at the bakery (turn to **41**)? If you are determined to have an afternoon off and to do nothing, turn to **428**.

203

You aim an Energy Bolt into the brown vapour. If you miss, turn to **153**. If you hit, the brown cloud swirls and begins to solidify as it drifts down to the ground. When it reaches the ground, it has reformed into the body of a dark-skinned man. You have captured the Smoke! However, you have not managed to prevent him sending radio photographs of the doctor's notes to the headquarters of F.E.A.R. Nevertheless, you may add 2 Hero Points for the arrest and turn to **162**.

204

As you summon up your power, the mutant's attention switches to you. You release the blast and Sidney Knox blinks. To your horror, it turns around in the air and heads back towards you, hitting you in the chest. You must lose 1 *SKILL* and 3 *STAMINA* points for this. You may now either rush in to attack him (turn to **33**), or back away to nurse your injury and leave the Lab (turn to **125**).

205

Extracting a Microlaser from your Accessory Belt, you step up to the car door to start to cut it open. 'Get out of it,' snaps an angry fireman. 'What're you trying to do, fancy pants? Put us all out of work? This is a job for professionals, not some peacock-costumed amateur!' You try to reason with the man, explaining that your Microlaser will do the job in half the time it would take him. 'Okay, hot shot,' he says. 'Let's see this fancy gizmo.' You flick the button. *Nothing happens!* Red-faced, you step back and let the firemen cut away the door. What a time for a malfunction! You sneak off into a side-alley, change clothes and walk back upstairs to work. Turn to **398**.

206

What password do you wish to try: *Peking Duck* (turn to **381**), or *Quicksilver* (turn to **130**)?

207

The Ringmaster leaps to a small door in the wall, opens it and jumps through it – straight into the lions' cage! An evil smile spreads across his lips as you follow him. Snapping a couple of words at the lions, he sends them towards you. If you have £ *TS*, turn to **92**. Otherwise turn to **297**.

208

You keep out of sight and follow the Macro Brain's movements. Although his forces are putting up a strong fight, the army is holding them back successfully. Your opportunity arises when the Macro Brain steals away into the Colonel's office. You are the only one who has noticed and you follow him there. If you have *Psi-Powers,* turn to **274**. If you have *ETS,* turn to **427**. If you have *Energy Blast,* turn to **392**.

209

You send a powerful submission blast of mental energy towards the figure behind the boxes. An anguished scream sounds from the thief. The foot twitches, then rests motionless. You step carefully over to investigate. Turn to **286**.

210

You withdraw a Sonic Confuser and prepare to use it on the gang. But an instant before they emerge, you realize this may not be such a good idea. There are too many innocent bystanders to be certain that your gadget will not harm them too. If you wish to use it anyway, turn to **406**. If you instead put it away and fight the Alchemists, turn to **243**.

211

Papers in his briefcase identify the man as Wayne Bruce, President of Euro-American Security Inc. There are also documents from his lawyer which relate to divorce proceedings. Other than these, there appears to be nothing else out of the ordinary in his case. Do you wish to visit his home to talk to his wife (turn to **195**), will you head for his office (turn to **233**), or will you leave this apparently simple, but brutal, mugging in the hands of the police (turn to **73**)?

212

Apart from making you large, small, fat, thin, long and short, the mirrors do not seem to hold any secrets. You are making little progress here. You overhear someone making comments about how dangerous he thinks the Big Dipper is. Will you go and check it out (turn to **187**), or is it time you were making for home (turn to **103**)?

213

Two dogs are not fully under your control. As you step into the room, they push past you and rush into the screaming crowd outside. Your first duty must be to deal with these beasts:

	SKILL	STAMINA
First RADIATION DOG	7	5
Second RADIATION DOG	6	5

Fight them one at a time. When one of the dogs first rolls a higher Attack Strength than you, turn to **31**. But before you do, *note this reference,* so you may return here afterwards. If you defeat both the escaped dogs, turn to **247**.

214

You come to a junction on the edge of Audubon Park. The only likely-looking buildings are on the north-east corner of the junction, where people are going in and out of a busy diner. Next to the diner is a pawnbroker's. Will you investigate the diner (turn to **351**) or the pawnbroker's (turn to **147**)?

An atmosphere of panic is in the air

215

In the morning, you set off for a stroll. As you turn the corner at the end of the block, the beeping from your wrist signifies the start of your busiest day yet. *'MURDOCK NUCLEAR LABORATORIES,'* speaks the message from your Crimewatch. You gulp: atomic weapons experiments are conducted at the Murdock Laboratories. Whatever is happening could be very serious indeed. You must get to the Murdock Labs without delay!

An atmosphere of panic is in the air when you arrive. A series of controlled radiation experiments were being conducted on animals to help determine the effects of a nuclear explosion. Some startling results had been achieved. Under certain conditions, distinct signs of increased mental powers were being shown by several of the experimental animals. Some of these were quite spectacular. They had, for example, produced a dog able to talk and a chimpanzee able to play computer games. But they had no doubt that similar experiments on humans would have produced much more dramatic results. This theory has now been proved true. Sidney Knox, one of the research assistants, had crept into the radiation chamber that morning and subjected himself to the rays. His brain is now twice its normal size and he has the ability to manipulate objects by *will-power alone!* But there is an unforeseen side-effect. Sidney

Knox, normally a peaceful individual, has developed a destructive streak. His powers enable him to will the radiation emitter to implode and destroy itself. The danger is if he gets anywhere near the nuclear reactor: destruction of the reactor would mean disaster on a grand scale for Titan City. No one knows where he is now, but the reactor must be protected at all costs. Where will you begin your search for the self-made mutant? At the nuclear reactor (turn to **343**) or around the test laboratories (turn to **377**)?

216

You concentrate hard. A dream-like vision shows the scene in the aircraft's cockpit. The Tormentor, shaggy-haired and cackling with a demonic laugh, has control of the plane. The pilot and co-pilot are bound hand and foot against one wall of the cockpit. The passengers are panicking and their screams only delight the madman. But what can you do from the ground? You may want to communicate telepathically with one of the passengers – someone who may be strong enough to grapple with the villain (turn to **308**). If you have another plan, turn to **176**.

217

Before she fell unconscious, your *Psi-Powers* picked up a strong feeling of fear. The Tiger Cat was thinking about a meeting that she couldn't afford to miss. Of course! F.E.A.R.! You concentrate your thoughts, but can only glimpse one piece of information before she blacks out. The meeting will be on 5th Avenue. But this is a long road. However, you can get no more information. Turn to **124**.

218

You make a promise to yourself. Tomorrow you are going to arrive at work *on time*. With that in mind, you can decide either to stay in and rest for the evening (turn to **337**), or go out to see a show. You have heard that 'Rats', the all-star musical by Lloyd Webber-Andrews, is playing to packed houses. If you fancy a night on the town, turn to **43**.

219

The cool air is refreshing and allows you to gather your thoughts. You must anticipate the F.E.A.R. meeting if you are to prevent their master-plan from succeeding. If only you knew where it was to be held, and... Thump! You feel a heavy blow across the back of your head and you drop to your knees. A rough accent says: 'Just get the money and let's get going. Quick!' A hand searches through your pockets for your cash. Though groggy, you know what is happening. You are being mugged! You could, if you wished, fight back, but that would mean you having to reveal your secret identity. Or you could let them think they have knocked you out – you have very little money on you, anyway. Will you fight back (turn to **230**), or let them rob you (turn to **279**)?

220

You wait for some time, but nothing happens. Eventually you give up. Puzzled about the whole affair, you decide to leave the airport and catch a taxi home. The driver has his radio on. As he chats away, the radio splutters and fizzles. The music dies and an unscheduled announcement interrupts the programme. Turn to **292**.

221

'Fear?' he laughs. 'Yes, I can tell you how to find fear. I found it myself. It must be going back ten years or more now. We were out in deep sea catching tunny. An' this storm, she swelled out of nowhere. Neptune's fury, we called it. Our ship was tossed about like a pea in a pot. Seven good men were lost overboard, and. . .' You listen to him politely, cursing silently to yourself. You *would* have to get stuck listening to some old fool's sea-stories. Turn to **368**.

222

A recent visitor from Metroville, the Tiger Cat has arrived in town. This extraordinary villainess is a fierce fighter, but can instantly disguise herself as a harmless pussy cat.

223

You approach a grand caravan painted in gay colours. There is no reply when you knock on the door, so you push it open. Inside, the caravan is tastefully decorated and photographs of circus acts line the walls. But no one is about. You can leave the circus and go to either the zoo (turn to **408**) or the Natural History Museum (turn to **365**).

224

You reach forward to grab the girl. Your clutching fingers manage to catch hold of one of the straps on her dungarees. But the material is not strong. The strap breaks and the helpless girl plunges over the side of the carriage to her death! Panic breaks out and the riders' screams continue until the ride is over. Desolate, you decide you have had enough of Wisneyland. Turn to **103**.

225

As the bus comes into Radid Square, you notice an excited crowd of people gathered in the centre of the square. Will you investigate the disturbance (turn to **201**), or ignore it and continue back to work (turn to **435**)?

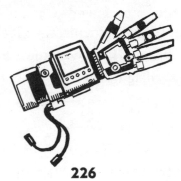

226

Where will you head for now? If you wish to make that visit to your aunt, turn to **134**. If you prefer to go downtown to see if you can get tickets for a special concert that Georgie Boy and the Vulture Club are giving, turn to **122**.

227

For capturing the Poisoner, you may award yourself 4 Hero Points. Before leaving the reservoir, you go through his pockets and come across an interesting clue. The Beast-King has escaped from jail and is planning a raid on Titan zoo. You note this information. Turn to **107**.

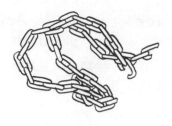

228

You study the newspaper. Under the headline *'ALCHEMISTS IN CLEVELAND'*, the story describes how the notorious gang of chemical experts entered a branch of the Cleveland Bank on 113th Street at 4 a.m., bypassed the alarm, locked the security guard in the vault on a time-switch and made off with a number of safe-deposit boxes. Although it was impossible to tell how much was taken in the raid, claims from the owners of the deposit boxes are now coming in. Apart from the cash, many valuable papers had been stolen. Do you want to investigate the robbery as the Silver Crusader (turn to **112**), or will you see what else is in the paper (turn to **386**)?

229

Sirens sound as first a fire-engine, then an ambulance, come racing round the corner. From the other direction, *another* ambulance arrives. The firemen get to work on cutting the doors away to release the occupants, both of whom are injured and suffering from shock. But the ambulance drivers are in the middle of a heated argument about who should pick up the patients! Meanwhile the fire has spread to the tank. The explosion that follows settles the ambulance drivers' dispute... You return to work upstairs. Turn to **398**.

230

One of them stuffs your money into his pocket, while the other is looking at your driving-licence, wondering whether or not he may be able to sell it. You leap to your feet and grapple with the muggers. One of them grabs the sweat-shirt you are wearing and it rips in his hand. Your heart sinks as the tear reveals your Crusader costume underneath it! The two muggers gasp: 'The Silver Crusader! Hey, er, sorry, Crusader. How were we to know it was you?' They give themselves up without a struggle and you hand them in at the local police station. But your career is over. Word of your true identity will soon get about from these two. And when it does, the lives of all your family and friends will be in danger from criminals seeking revenge. The time has come for you to hang up your cape...

231

You take out a vial of Concentrated Antifreeze and rush out into the centre of the ice. Removing the stopper, you pour it on to the ice around the two girls. A puddle of water spreads around them and their struggles allow them to move more freely. Moments later they are free and you help them to the side of the pool, where friends are waiting with warm blankets. You may add 2 Hero Points for the rescue, then you must leave the pool (turn to **362**). But you may, if you wish, check the heating-plant first before you go (turn to **347**).

232

You creep silently over to the boxes. In a single motion, you grab the foot and heave the fugitive from his hiding-hole. But when you see what you have caught, your anger rises. The thief can be no more than nine years old! A young boy, still clutching his booty – a half-eaten Goo Bar – looks up at you with terrified eyes! You grab his wrist and march him inside. Turn to **316**.

233

At the offices of Euro-American Security, the staff are shocked to hear of their Presidents murder. Wayne Bruce's secretary, an attractive blonde with dark eyes, introduces you to the company's senior executives. But none can shed any light on why anyone should want to murder their boss. You decide that the incident must have been the mugging it seemed and that you will leave it to the police. Turn to **73**.

234

You react immediately and swing the wheel full circle, taking your foot off the pedal at the same time. Your car lurches and stops dead. Although *you* have avoided hitting the boy, the woman in Purple 10 does not have the same speed of reaction. Her car hits the boy, who drops unconscious to the ground. The power stops immediately and a crowd of people, led by the boy's shrieking mother, flood on to the track. The boy is still breathing. An ambulance arrives to take him to hospital. You are feeling somewhat shocked by the near-disaster and decide you have had enough of Wisneyland for the day. Turn to **103**.

235

Your hands drop, as if in submission to his orders. Your right hand moves towards a pouch on your Accessory Belt.

'Not so fast, Crusader!' the Poisoner warns. 'Touch that belt and this vial disappears into the water supply.' He has spotted your plan. Turn to **25**.

236

Quick as a flash, you fly out over the roof, come up in front of the man and hit him with a blow that knocks the gun out of his hand. He falls back on to the roof and you must resolve your battle with him:

ASSASSIN   *SKILL 9*   *STAMINA 8*

If you defeat him, turn to **258**.

237

You step up to the door and wait for the frantic barking to die down. It does not. In fact the dogs are clawing and jumping at the door, which is beginning to weaken. You grasp the handle and prepare to rush in. Roll one die. If you roll 1–4, turn to **132**. If you roll 5 or 6, turn to **375**.

When you arrive at the house, a young boy opens the door. 'Wow!' he gasps. 'The Silver Crusader come to see us! Er . . . if you want to see my dad, he's not in. But you can come in, anyway.' You explain that it's *him* you want to see and you ask whether he's had any interesting dreams recently. He tells you about this 'really neat' one he's just had about a huge green monster rising out of a fountain and attacking people. Your suspicions were correct. This is the 'Brain Child' you were warned about. His dreams are so vivid that they actually come to life. His mother appears and you explain the situation. She will see that he is taken to a hospital immediately for treatment. You have saved the city from any number of possible disasters here. Add 3 Hero Points. His mother tells you that her son sometimes has premonitions of the future. He was talking the other day about something that might be important. Apparently a man in control of wild animals was using them to get some sort of revenge. He had a secret room under a lion's cage with a special trapdoor leading from it. With this information you can search for such a secret room, if you arrive at a lion's cage, by adding 50 to the reference you are on at the time and turning to this new reference. You may add 1 *LUCK* point for this information. Leave when you are ready and return to Radd Square (turn to **71**).

239

There is no one about to help you. What can you do? Simply leave the creature where it lies? You decide the best thing to do is to place it back in its grave and cover it until you can bring the police to dispose of the Reincarnation more effectively. You cannot gain any Hero Points for this encounter, as no one has seen you defeat it! Such are the rewards of a devotion to public service... Now you continue by setting off once more for your aunt's. Turn to **76**.

240

The Princess's sarcophagus, in all its splendour, is watched by three security guards. Priceless golden treasures adorn the exhibit. There is no doubt that any of these would make rich pickings for a thief. You talk to the guards and compare the exhibit with its description in the catalogue. All seems to be in order. It seems that you are wasting your time here, and you decide to leave. Turn to **276**.

241

The police arrive to take care of the Ice Queen. You may add 4 Hero Points for capturing her and then you must leave the abattoir. Turn to **362**.

It is destroying everything in sight

242

A huge crowd has gathered round Titan City Library. The police are struggling to keep them away from the building to allow both the army and the fire-brigade to get closer. What is happening? Your question is answered when a third-floor window smashes. The smash is followed by screams as two bodies come hurtling out of the broken window, followed by a huge bookshelf. Books and glass rain down on the terrified crowds. Inside you can hear a roar which chills you to the bone. The police chief is glad to see you. 'We need help, Crusader,' he pleads. 'Some sort of creature is inside there. They've called it the Devastator. Looks like something not of this earth! A huge brute – I'd say it's made from rock!' You rush into the building and find the creature on the third floor. Your jaw drops. Indeed, it does seem to be made from rock rather than living flesh, and it stands some four metres high. Something has enraged it and it is destroying everything in sight, pushing over huge shelves of books and smashing tables and chairs. If you have *Super Strength,* turn to **378**. If you have *ETS,* turn to **421**. If you have *Psi-Powers,* turn to **192**. If you have *Energy Blast,* turn to **363**. If you don't think you can handle this creature, you can leave by turning to **319**.

243

As the three Alchemists emerge from the bank, you charge into them. Fight the three of them one at a time:

	SKILL	STAMINA
First ALCHEMIST	8	6
Second ALCHEMIST	7	7
Third ALCHEMIST	7	6

If you defeat them all, turn to **336**.

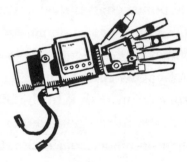

244

The firemen get to work on cutting the doors away to release the occupants, both of whom are injured and suffering from shock. But the ambulance drivers are in the middle of a heated argument about who should pick up the patients! Meanwhile the fire has spread to the tank. The explosion that follows settles the ambulance drivers' dispute... You step back into a side-street, change costume and return to work upstairs. Lose 1 Hero Point and turn to **398**.

245

Lieutenant Wojak shakes your hand enthusiastically as you enter police headquarters. 'Crusader! Hi! Good to see you. Come into my office. . .' He tells you that, apart from the usual muggings, break-ins and auto-thefts, he has just had some disturbing news. There has been a well-organized jail break at Woodworm Scrubs, the high-security prison. Marcus Buletta, who was serving a fourteen-year sentence, climbed over the wall with a rope-ladder and escaped in a waiting van disguised as an ambulance. Also, Central Hospital has just reported a strange admission, someone named Winston Woods, whose head and hands are rough and hairy, like those of a great ape. Do you wish to investigate the strange case at the hospital (turn to **190**), will you go shopping (turn to **94**), or will you tell the police to keep you informed and go to visit your aunt (turn to **134**)?

246

You scan the minds of the people in the shop. They are not lying; they know nothing about the kidnapping. However, while you are there, the delivery-boy comes up into the shop from downstairs. His mind has a rather different aura about it. In fact, as he arrives, his mind is not on his job. He is thinking of an important meeting. Reading his mind, you can picture a street corner: the sign reads '209th Street'. And a final image makes you glare hard at the boy. The emblem of F.E.A.R. flashes up in his mind! But what has such a youngster to do with F.E.A.R.? When he realizes what you are up to, he dashes out into the street. You rush after him, but he is very quick. Moments later, he has disappeared, leaving you to puzzle over his thoughts. What will you do now? If the millionaire is inside the runaway van, you cannot hope to catch it – but you could phone the details through to the police and hope that they can track it down; then turn to **428**. Otherwise you can search for other clues outside the shop (turn to **331**).

247

You must now return to the Lab to fight however many dogs remain. Turn to **120**.

248

If you want to check some of the special attractions of the Fun House, turn to **143**. Alternatively, you may know exactly where you want to look. If this is the case, you will know how to get there and you may go there immediately.

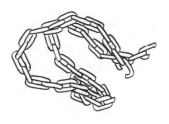

249

You are powerless to prevent the aircraft taking off. Cursing, you turn back to the airport: you can do nothing but inform the authorities. But you are aware that this will be of little use, as the jet will no doubt have arranged some secret landing-field. You catch a taxi home. The driver has his radio on. As he chats away, the radio splutters and fizzles. The music dies and an unscheduled announcement interrupts the programme. Turn to **292**.

250

You enter the room and interrupt a struggle. Lola Manche is punching and kicking her would-be kidnapper, who is attempting to push her out of the window to escape from the theatre! Judging by the mess all around the dressing-room – clothes are strewn about and jars of make-up lie broken on the floor – the struggle has been going on for some time, but the Serpent has almost succeeded in getting her through the window. You must leap in quickly before it is too late:

THE SERPENT   *SKILL 8*   *STAMINA 8*

The Serpent has a powerful secret weapon – his poisonous bite. Each time he hits you, roll one die. A roll of 1 or 2 indicates a bite and the poison will take effect. Deduct 1 *SKILL* point each time you are bitten. However, the effects of the bite are only temporary. You will recover your *SKILL* after one full day. If you defeat the villain, turn to **432**.

251

You hand the medallion to the officer who places it in a small plastic bag. 'Seems to me like just another mugging,' he says. 'But it's very strange. It happened in broad daylight and the guy's wallet hasn't even been touched. Anyway, thanks for your help.' You leave the area, once you have changed into your street clothes. Turn to **181**.

252

As you climb down inside the submarine, a noise from within alerts you. It is the dull clanking of metal on metal. But it sounds also like another familiar sound. *Footsteps!* You quickly climb down inside and search for a convenient hiding-spot. The door to a small chamber is open and you nip inside. Moments later, you can hear the sound of more footsteps and a human figure stops outside your chamber. 'Which numbskull left the door to the ejection chamber open?' he says, spinning the handle to lock you inside. Your heart sinks. The *ejection chamber?* You are trapped. How will you escape? You must try to use your power:

Super Strength	Turn to **390**
Psi-Powers	Turn to **59**
ETS	Turn to **145**
Energy Blast	Turn to **6**

253

The curator takes you round the stuffed exhibits. Gorillas, rhinos, great cats, even a whale – they are all there and you examine them with interest. Two in particular catch your attention. One of the tigers has dried blood on its claws, but there is no way of knowing whether the blood is human or animal, or even how long it has been there. Also, the curator tells you that the elephant was moved into the ground-floor private exhibit rooms yesterday for cleaning. If you want to pursue your investigations with these exhibits, turn to **161**. If you wish to have a look at the dinosaurs, turn to **345**.

254

At the gates, the security guard says he remembers the car leave, but he didn't see who was driving. The car did indeed head towards Titan City centre. But how will you track it down? You inform the police to look out for its licence-plate number and leave the Murdock Laboratories. Turn to **125**.

255

The Bolt misses. You do not have time to try another shot, as the shark is dangerously near the young boy. If you miss again, the boy is doomed. Wisely, you decide to spring into the water and grapple with the shark. Turn to **294**.

'Terror ... the little terror!'

256

Quick as a flash, you spring into the shop ready for action. It is a small sweets, candies and tobacco shop. The proprietor, a Mr Kalvin Farquarson, is standing behind the counter in a state of shock, his head buried in his hands. You shake his shoulders and tell him to pull himself together. He composes himself and stammers: 'Terror! The little terror...! Pulled a gun ... grabbed everything on the counter ... and ran out through there!' He points through the shop to what is apparently the back door. Will you race for the back door to stop the thief before he can get away (turn to **24**), or will you grab something to use as cover first (turn to **101**)?

257

Your wait is brief. The doctor comes downstairs in his dressing-gown and wants to know what you want. You explain your clue and how you feel that someone may be trying to steal his secrets. He is not impressed and takes you into his study to show you that nothing is amiss. Turn to **303**.

258

You pick the assassin up by the collar and demand to know who he is working for. He realizes that the game is up and admits that he works for F.E.A.R.! You threaten him with more punishment unless he tells you the whereabouts of the meeting you know is about to take place, but he swears he knows nothing more than that it is due to take place tomorrow. Perhaps he is telling the truth. You hand him over to the police and head for home. You have saved the President's life and may award yourself 6 Hero Points. Turn to **311**.

259

You try talking to the security guard, but it is no use. The vault is over a metre thick and he cannot hear you. While you are trying, however, you do find out what has happened. The Alchemists, masters of advanced chemistry, had neutralized the alarm with some sort of acidic gas which delayed its being activated as they forced their way in. Another unknown compound had dissolved the security lock on the main door. Why the security guard had not noticed the intruders was still a mystery which would only be solved when the time-lock released him from the vault. You may, if you wish, try to smash the vault door to release the guard. If you have *Energy Blast,* turn to **183**; otherwise turn to **5**. If, on the other hand, you see this as a futile exercise, turn to **60**.

260

You seem to be getting through to the demented maniac. You try a different tack, telling him to think of his wife or his girl-friend, and how she will feel if he crashes the plane. His anger rises! He switches off the radio and you watch despairingly as the plane lurches in the air and plummets down towards the edge of the landing-field. Helplessly, you watch the plane crash into the ground. There will be no survivors. Turn to **10**.

261

You knock the Fire Warrior backwards. He lands unconscious in a pile on the floor and his flames die out. Now you must go for the other three. As it takes only a low-level Energy Bolt to knock them out, you may fire at each one. When you have hit two of them, turn to **53**.

262

The creature spies you and swings a great fist. Resolve this battle:

THE DEVASTATOR   *SKILL 14*   *STAMINA 12*

If you win, turn to **119**.

263

Do you wish to step into the crowd in street clothes (turn to **99**), or nip round a corner to change into the Silver Crusader (turn to **191**)?

264

The sales assistants are all demonstrating various machines to other customers and you wander round looking at the racks of software. You take a copy of a 'Whack Man' variant and study the description on the box. 'I don't rate that one myself,' says a voice behind you. You turn round. It is Gerry the Grass! You must be careful not to give yourself away, for he doesn't know you as Jean Lafayette. You chat away to him and he tells you of his hobbies: computers, CB radio and amateur detective work. As he boasts of his interests, he gives you some information. Apparently he has heard of a plot to assassinate the President, who is due to arrive in Titan City tomorrow on a visit. There will be a decoy gunman in the crowd, but the real killer will be on the roof of the Regent Hotel. He tried to tell the police, but they dismissed him as a crank. With this information, you may apprehend the gunman by adding 100 to the reference you are on when you arrive on 7th Avenue and turning to that reference. You thank him for his advice on the game and leave. Turn to **226**.

265

Your blast hits the creature square in the chest. It roars ...
and then vanishes! Your jaw drops. What is happening
here? Likewise, the watching crowds are completely
baffled. Turn to **138**.

266

A Chinaman jabbers at you as you walk in. 'Yes, yes,
yes?' he asks. He is obviously in a hurry. Will you push
past him and look around the shop (turn to **334**), or do
you have a password you would like to try on him (turn
to **206**)?

267

The firemen cut through the car door. When the
door is freed, you help bend it open and grab the two
passengers, pulling them to safety away from the
flaming car. An instant later, the tank catches fire and
explodes, but all the onlookers are a safe distance away.
Not a particularly dramatic rescue, but nevertheless
you have helped save their lives. Leaving them with
the ambulance-men, you walk away from the crowd to
find a suitable hiding-place and change into your street
clothes. You may award yourself 1 Hero Point for the
rescue, before climbing the stairs back to your office.
Turn to **398**.

268

You explain to the manager of the drug store that you are looking for clues which will help you locate the Poisoner. He is happy to let you look round his shop and investigate the storerooms downstairs. But you can find no evidence of the Poisoner's presence. You thank the manager for his help and leave. You have no leads to follow up. Turn to **107**.

269

You grab the flask and hurl it out of the window. This was not a good choice. First of all the flask was hot and has severely burned your hand – lose 1 *SKILL* point. Secondly, the contents of the bottle have splashed over passers-by on the ground below. For this you must lose 2 Hero Points. Nevertheless, you have prevented the explosion. The Professor thanks you for averting what could have been a disaster. You leave the building and head for home. Turn to **18**.

270

At the mention of his name, your eyes fall on Mustapha Kareem. He holds your gaze, then breaks away, nervously. You grab his shoulder and ask him to answer a few questions. To the great surprise of the curator, Kareem breaks free and rushes off downstairs into the vaults of the museum, with you hot in pursuit. You catch up with him in a dimly lit room in which several wooden crates stand. Kareem is cornered. But as you advance, a wicked smile spreads across his lips. His skin begins to wither. His eyes become sunken pits in their sockets. He stands before you as a *Mummy* and raises his arms as he comes towards you to attack. If you have *Energy Blast,* turn to **170**. If you have *Super Strength,* turn to **109**. Otherwise, turn to **61**.

271

With a miniature Sensor Scanner, you examine the man's pocket for clues. The scanner indicates some flakes of skin from a hand that was not his own. Something strange is going on here! Turn to **143**.

272

"You fly into the air and smack your fist into the creature's jaw. It drops its victim into the water and a red stain spreads around the body. You now have a fight on your hands:

FOUNTAIN CREATURE   *SKILL 10*   *STAMINA 11*

When you inflict your fourth wound on the beast, turn to **65**.

273

Turn to **34**.

274

You confront the villain in the Colonel's office. He is startled to see you appear, and turns to face you. 'So!' he smiles. 'The Silver Crusader, as always, fights on the side of what is good and just. Sickening. But perhaps that can be changed...' What follows is a contest of will – yours against that of the Macro Brain, who has similar powers. But the Macro Brain has been waiting for this. He has not had such a busy day, and his powerful mind begins to prevail. You break out in a sweat from the exertion and finally drop to your knees in submission. But your foe has not finished yet. 'Crusader,' he announces, 'for many years you have fought for justice. From now on you will become servant to the Macro Brain!' You feel your will slipping. He has overpowered you and is now implanting mental suggestions. Your struggles are to no avail. No longer will you be Titan City's avenger against evil. Instead you are destined to become a useful pawn to the immense intelligence that is the Macro Brain...

275

You summon up your energy and try another Bolt. Again the effort is tiring and you must lose another 2 STAMINA points. But this time you manage to burn through to the door-mechanism, and a metallic clang sounds from within. The door swings slightly ajar and you enter the vault. Deposit boxes are strewn about the floor and in the centre, lying spread-eagled, is the security guard. Blood trickles from a nasty gash on his forehead. This injury, together with the lack of fresh air in the vault, has been too much for him. As you kneel down beside him, he is gasping his last breaths. Seeing you, he whispers a few dying words, interrupted by coughs, into your ear: 'Alchemists... Overheard meeting plans... Big deal... Nervous... Fear... Submarine... Ahhhhhh...' His head falls to one side: the man is dead. Turn to **60**.

276

Where to now? You may want to visit the Titan Central Library to do some research in their criminology section (turn to **242**), or you could go to visit Gerry the Grass (turn to **38**).

277

Silently you climb the stairs. Four steps from the top, your foot creaks on the old wooden board. The voices upstairs fall silent. They have heard the noise. Drat! You look up to see two sights, neither of which is comforting. Above the stairs is a mirror. The Mantrapper and his men have without doubt noticed you. The second thing you see is a pipe suspended over the stairs, its open end pointing straight at you. As you watch it, a whiff of green smoke puffs out of the pipe into your face. You cough heavily. Another of the Mantrapper's little traps, no doubt – and one from which you will not recover, as you take the poison gas into your lungs. Your valiant attempt to save the millionaire has been in vain.

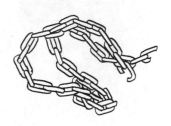

278

The Cats' Home is not far from the Dairy. As if it senses where it is going, the little animal squirms to get free. It fights and scratches in your grip. It seems to be getting heavier! Suddenly a remarkable transformation takes place. You drop the cat to the ground and before your eyes it grows in size and takes on a female human form, until it stands before you as the Tiger Cat! *Of course!* This wicked she-villain has a record of robbing dairies and fish factories. Her tight, tiger-striped costume has sharp claws at the hands and feet and she springs at you:

TIGER CAT   *SKILL 9*   *STAMINA 8*

If you have *Psi-Powers,* turn to **413**. If you have *ETS,* turn to **168**. You have no time to use an Energy Bolt. If you defeat the Tiger Cat, turn to **124**.

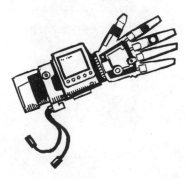

279

You fake unconsciousness and, seething inwardly, let them take the money that they are after. A car pulls up and they leap inside, cursing about how little they have taken. You memorize the number: the police can handle this one. Lose 2 *STAMINA* points for the blow on the head, and turn to **76**.

280

Recently you have learned the true identities of several of the crime world's most notorious super-villains. The Tormentor has been identified as Richard Storm, an uptown heating engineer. The Ice Queen is none other than Sylvia Frost, society debutante. And Marcus Buletta is known to be the gruesome Dr Macabre, whose terrible experiments in surgery have shocked the world. Buletta has been planning a jail-break for months. When he does so, he is likely to rob a chemist immediately for surgical equipment and chemicals.

281

You sit down next to a kid listening to a Walkman and borrow it to listen to the tape. It seems to be a recording of a telephone conversation between a man and a woman. The conversation ends: 'Don't worry. The treasures are being collected and replaced by our agent, Mustapha Kareem. We will have them all soon. Remember, we meet the day after tomorrow on board the yacht. Okay. Bye.' Interesting stuff.

This Mustapha Kareem sounds like a dubious character. If you come across him, you may question him about his activities by doubling the reference number you are on at the time and turning to this new reference. Add 1 *LUCK* point for discovering this message, and turn to **86**.

282

There is no other course of action you can take but to grapple with the berserk Android:

ANDROID   *SKILL 9*   *STAMINA 11*

After the second round of combat, turn to **335**.

283

You jump over the counter and quickly change costume. When you step forwards as the Silver Crusader, the Fire Warriors stop in their tracks. You warn them and order them to give themselves up. But your words are wasted. One of them lunges for you and you will have to release an Energy Bolt. If you hit, turn to **261**. If you miss, turn to **200**.

Four Alsatian dogs have escaped from their cages

284

You quickly change into the Silver Crusader and rush to the Peter Laboratories. It is near the centre of town, annexed to the nuclear physics department of the university. When you arrive, you are sent straight upstairs to the third floor, but told to be careful. A group of students and professors are huddled by the stairs. You are told what has happened. Four Alsatian dogs which were being used in dangerous radiation experiments have escaped from their cages. They are locked in a room down the corridor and are barking wildly. Although they should not be radioactive to the touch, their bite could be lethal, should their saliva enter an open cut.

If you survive this episode, you may award yourself 1 Hero Point for each of the dogs you capture, but you must deduct 1 Hero Point for each person who is bitten by a dog. If you have:

ETS	Turn to **328**
Energy Blast	Turn to **306**
Psi-Powers	Turn to **105**
Super Strength	Turn to **237**

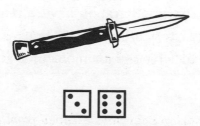

285

You watch from the control tower as the Tormentor steps out of the plane and gives himself up to the police, who are waiting on the runway. The Air-Traffic Controller thanks you for your help, and you leave. You may add 2 Hero Points. Turn to **10**.

286

You grab the unconscious thief and pull him out from behind the boxes. As he slides out into the daylight, you gulp. This little villain can be no more than nine years old! You may well have hurt him badly! In his right hand he clutches his booty – a half-eaten Goo Bar. Desperately, you shake him, and eventually his eyes flick open. He is terrified to see you and you scowl at him sternly. But secretly you are relieved that he is not seriously hurt. You pick him up and march inside the shop. Turn to **316**.

287

You first of all try to latch on to the mind of the arch-criminal you know to be inside the brown cloud. This is difficult, but you do find out one thing. He has been taking pictures of the doctor's notes with a radio camera and the photographs have already been sent to the headquarters of F.E.A.R.! Then you concentrate hard, trying to alter the air molecules around the gas to imprison the villain. But it is no use. You have failed to prevent important secrets from reaching the eyes of F.E.A.R. Turn to **162**.

288

You push the door open and step into an untidy dressing-room. Clothes are strewn about the floor and jars of make-up lie open on the dressing-table in front of the mirror. But otherwise the room is empty. You search through the mess for a clue to the Serpent's whereabouts, but find nothing. Do you want to try room number one (turn to **322**) or room number three (turn to **117**) instead?

289

As you enter the park, you pick up sounds of a commotion and follow it to a crowd grouped around a body. Police are trying to move the crowd on. Will you push through to see what is happening (turn to **434**), or change into the Silver Crusader (turn to **104**)?

290

Are you anticipating this meeting? If so, you will know what time you ought to arrive to catch the meeting in progress. Add this time to today's date (do you know what this is?) and turn to the reference corresponding to this number. If the resulting reference makes no sense, turn to **368**.

291

'Escaped animals?' she asks. 'I don't *think* any of our animals have escaped. But I'll just check for you, if you like.' She picks up a land-line telephone and cranks a handle. 'Hello, Mario? This is Nancy. Someone here wants to know whether any animals have escaped... No, I didn't think so. Thanks. Bye.' She shakes her head and you leave. Where will you try now? You can try the zoo (turn to **408**) or the Natural History Museum (turn to **365**).

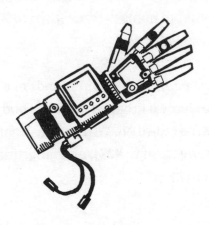

292

A steely voice with a sinister tone speaks slowly and clearly: 'Citizens of the world,' it announces, 'do not attempt to retune your receivers. This message is being broadcast on all frequencies simultaneously in all languages to all areas of the globe. My name is

Vladimir Utoshski. I am known as the Titanium Cyborg. My organization is known to you as the Federation of Euro-American Rebels. My message is this. We have taken control of the "Star Wars" satellite which orbits the earth. We demand the unconditional surrender of all your governments and military establishments and the submission of all citizens to our leadership. Any resistance will be dealt with harshly. Our satellite will obliterate, one by one, the major cities of the earth. As proof of our power, Titan City will be exterminated in exactly thirty seconds...' Your heart sinks. You have failed to stop the fateful meeting of F.E.A.R. The whole world must now pay the penalty...

293

You sneak away from the waiting crowd, change costume and make for home. You have had an exhausting day and you slump in front of the TV with a long, cold drink. You may add 6 *STAMINA* points for the rest. The next morning you leave for work early. You catch a bus, but to refresh yourself before work, you get off and walk the last half of the journey. Typical: as soon as you get off the bus, it starts to rain! You begin to run but slow down when you arrive at Cowfield Dairy. Something is not quite right. Do you wish to investigate (turn to **369**), or are you already on your way to somewhere more important? If so, you will know how to get there.

294

With a tremendous splashing, the fight commences:

RIPPER SHARK   *SKILL 10*   *STAMINA 8*

When the shark has inflicted its fourth wound on you, turn to **95**. If you defeat the shark before it has inflicted four wounds, turn to **197**.

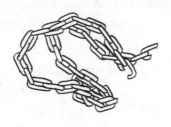

295

From your Accessory Belt you draw an Absolute Zero Flask. Quickly, you step over to the experiment and bring the flask up to surround the bottle. Moments later, the danger is over. The liquid in the bottle has frozen, and will do no further harm. The Professor thanks you for saving the lives of everyone in the building. You may add 1 Hero Point. You leave and make for home. Turn to **18**.

296

You go through the man's pockets to retrieve the wallet. He is carrying some peculiar things, no doubt the pickings of his trade. Along with the wallet, you find a cigarette packet which contains a crumpled piece of paper, a tape cassette and a map. Before handing the pickpocket over to a security guard on the train, you manage to take *one* of these from him. Which did you take? The cigarette packet (turn to **423**), the cassette tape (turn to **281**) or the map (turn to **20**)?

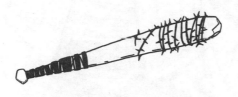

297

You will have to do battle with the lions. If you can defeat them, the Ringmaster will give himself up:

	SKILL	STAMINA
First LION	8	9
Second LION	7	8

Fight them one at a time. If you defeat them both, turn to **433**.

'This puny specimen is no match for the Titanium Cyborg!

You burst through the door into a smoke-filled room. Six startled faces wheel round to stare at you from their seats around a conference table. You recognize them all as agents of F.E.A.R. At the head of the table sits a man whose face you could never forget. The bald head, pointed nose and eye-goggles belong to Vladimir Utoshski, leader of F.E.A.R. He rises to his feet and speaks: 'So! The Silver Crusader honours us with a visit. Could it be that you wish to join us? I think not. My friends, I will show you how F.E.A.R. must deal with its enemies. This puny specimen is no match for the Titanium Cyborg!' The half-human, half-mechanical man steps towards you, his two electro-assisted arms ready to attack. A glowing light pulses in the goggles he uses for eyes. Do you have a Circuit Jammer with you? If so, turn to **159**. If not, you will have to fight the leader of F.E.A.R.:

TITANIUM CYBORG   *SKILL* 18   *STAMINA* 20

After the third round of combat, turn to **136**.

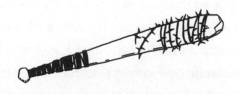

299

You rush to the edge of the water and search the surface for the tell-tale fin of a shark. Thirty metres out from the shore, you spot it. A monster! Swimming in towards the beach is a huge ripper shark! It is heading straight for a young boy who is still on his way back to the beach. What a nuisance! You could easily have seen the shark off with your Omnidirectional Electrifier. But with the boy in the way, you cannot risk using it. You will have to plunge into the water and tackle the shark with your bare hands. Turn to **294**.

300

As you step up to Epiphany's window, you notice a familiar figure taking an unhealthy interest in the diamond rings – Porcelain Percy, so called because his punishment for once betraying a former boss was to have all his teeth filed down to the gums and they all had to be built up with porcelain caps. He stands aside nervously as you step up to the window. You play with him a little. Did he not have something to do with the smash-and-grab at De Lager's jeweller's last week? Wasn't he seen talking to Timmy the Tongue? Maybe it would be better for all if you were to just hand him over to Big Ben and the Slicer; it would save the police a lot of effort… Porcelain Percy starts to sweat profusely and agrees to give you some information if you will just forget you have even seen him. Apparently he knows that the Poisoner has plans which threaten the lives of all the inhabitants of Titan City.

He also tells you more about what the Poisoner's plans are. If you find yourself searching for the Poisoner, deduct 30 from the reference you are on when you are given the opportunity, and turn to this new reference. You may add 1 *LUCK* point for this information. Then you allow the skinny little man to go home. The rest of the evening is uneventful and you get a good night's rest. You may add 6 *STAMINA* points. Turn to **327**.

301

'Lafayette! Get in here *at once!*' No sooner had you stepped through the office door than Jonah Whyte's booming voice summoned you. You creep into his office, mumbling scanty excuses for being late yet again. 'Enough!' he yells. 'What do you think we are running here? A charity? Do you suppose I should be grateful that you even grace us with your presence? Very noble of you indeed to even bother coming in at all! Well, I tell you what. I'm feeling kind today. You can have the rest of the day off. *Without pay!* And if you're not in first thing tomorrow morning, you can start looking for another job!' You slink out of his office with your tail between your legs. How can you tell him what you've been doing? And now you've been suspended for a day. Where will you go? Will you spend the day at Wisneyland, the amusement park (turn to **15**), or will you avoid all contact with the outside world and go home to make sure you get an early start in the morning (turn to **218**)?

302

After a brief snack, they get up and leave the diner. You overheard part of their conversation, but their heated discussions were no more than arguments about the likely results of tomorrow's horse-races. You are wasting your time. You leave the diner and catch a cab. Turn to **368**.

303

'There, you see!' says the doctor as you enter the study. 'All is in order. Just as I left it.' But you are not listening. Your attention has been caught by a dark whisp of brown smoke that is passing out of the window through the air-conditioner. You race quickly outside. Turn to **29**.

304

You prepare to use *Energy Blast* on the Android, but decide that you cannot risk it with so many innocent people about. What can you do against the creature? The answer comes from a man in the crowd who has been watching the demonstration. 'Try this,' he shouts, throwing you a small pen-like device. 'The demonstrator was asked what happens if the Android becomes uncontrollable and showed us this. He called it a "Circuit Jammer" or something. Maybe it will help.' You catch the device and hold it to the Android. Sure enough, the little gadget lives up to its name and the movements of the Android cease. You may add 4 Hero

Points for defeating the Android and you may also take the strange little device with you. Having seen enough of the exhibition, you decide to leave Whirl's Court. Turn to **75**.

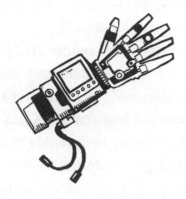

305

The police officers help you over to a bench. You overhear their conversation: 'Ugly incident in Audubon, seems like. Throat slashed. Made a mess of the path...' The other replies, 'Yeah. And Cleveland Bank. They reckon that was the Alchemists. Glad I wasn't the night-watchman when *they* came in!' The two nod in agreement. 'Looks like things are hotting up,' says the first, as they walk back to their yellow and black car. What will you do now? You could walk into Audubon Park to see what they were talking about (turn to **165**), buy a paper to see if you can pick up any news on the robbery (turn to **228**), or go to work (turn to **341**).

306

You may use *Energy Blast* against the dogs only in the confines of the Lab. If a dog escapes into the crowd, you dare not risk using it. Turn to **237**.

307

What can you do to help the swimmers? An Energy Bolt would melt the ice around them, but you cannot risk hitting the girls. However, you could aim a Bolt in a ring around them. This will cost you 4 *STAMINA* points, as it will have to be a prolonged effort. If you decide to help them, you can add 2 Hero Points. If you don't want to deplete your *STAMINA,* you must *lose* 2 Hero Points and face the boos of the onlookers as you walk away. Turn to **362** to leave.

308

Using your mental powers, you search quickly through the passengers. A burly man with wide shoulders catches your attention. You make contact with him and will him towards the cockpit to take on the Tormentor. He shakes his head and stares into the distance as he listens to your message. Suddenly he springs up from his seat. *'Hallelujah!'* he cries. 'I have received the word of the Lord! I must rid us of this unbeliever. My mission has been sent from above!' Your heart sinks. Just what you needed – a religious fanatic who thinks your message is some sort of divine omen. In your mind's eye you watch as he stomps forwards up the aisle towards the cockpit, giving the Tormentor full warning of his approach. The villain throws the joystick forwards and sends the plane into a deep dive. Unconcerned about his own life, he has made sure that his plan will succeed. Moments later, the plane crashes to the ground, killing all on board. Your plan has failed. You leave the airport. Turn to **10**.

309

You wait anxiously for the Alchemists to emerge from the bank. Passers-by are not aware of what is happening, but you manage to prevent any from entering while the robbery is in progress. However, you cannot avoid the curiosity of the public. One small boy strains on his mother's arm and yells out: 'Mommy, look! It's the Silver Crusader! Can I ask for an autograph, mommy? Please, mommy, can I?' You try to hush him up, but only manage to annoy his mother. Unaware of the situation, she thinks you are extremely rude. Have the boy's cries alerted the Alchemists? *Test your Luck.* If you are Lucky, turn to **128**. If you are Unlucky, turn to **155**.

310

There are two lions inside the cage. They are lying contentedly on the floor, licking their paws as if they had just finished a meal. But there are no signs of meat in the cage. Several metres from the cage is an elephant tied to a stake. These beasts could well be the killers, but what evidence do you have? Do you want to arrest the lion-tamer and take him to police headquarters (turn to **383**), or will you try to gather more evidence (turn to **45**). If you have *Psi-Powers,* turn to **321**.

311

You set off home to take some well-deserved rest. The prospect of the F.E.A.R. meeting is weighing heavily on your mind, but for the moment you are well advised to relax for the evening. You may gain 6 *STAMINA* points for taking it easy. Next morning, you are woken, not by the alarm clock, but by your Crimewatch: *beep – beep – beep.*

This time the message is longer than normal and it repeats itself: *'RELIABLE INFORMATION, FEAR MEETING TODAY. WHEREABOUTS UNKNOWN!'* You spring out of bed. *Today!* Do you have any clues as to where the meeting is? Where will you go:

Parker Airport?	Turn to **349**
Stay in town?	Turn to **70**
Head towards the waterfront?	Turn to **290**

312

The President is due to pay a visit to Titan City. Rumours are going round that an attempt will be made on his life when he arrives. It would be wise to find out how this attempt will be made. Both Marcus Buletta and Rat-face Flanagan know how the attempt will be made.

One has four arms and is snatching bottles from the shelves

313

As you are about to enter the drug store, you hear screams from inside. You nip into a storeroom and change into the Silver Crusader to investigate the disturbance. When you rush into the shop, you see two figures rummaging through the pharmaceutical shelves, while a crowd of terrified onlookers are held at bay by another. You recognize him as Dr Macabre, the mad surgeon whose brilliant experiments in transplant surgery were outlawed by a world not yet ready for the advances he had made. His two henchmen are the results of his work. One has four arms and is snatching bottles from the shelves with them. The other has the head of a tiger and is terrorizing the shop staff with his sharp teeth. You leap into action. If you have *ETS,* turn to **325**. If you have *Psi-Powers,* turn to **173**. If you have *Super Strength,* turn to **78**. If you have *Energy Blast,* turn to **142**.

314

You race out of the vaults and back upstairs where you tell the curator what has happened and leave the affair in his hands. You must deduct 2 Hero Points for leaving prematurely. Turn to **276**.

315

You fly up in the air and come down with a mighty *thump* in the creature's chest. The blow winds it and it temporarily releases the girders and turns its attention to you. Resolve this battle:

CREATURE OF CARNAGE   *SKILL 12*   *STAMINA 14*

If you defeat the Creature of Carnage, turn to **131**.

316

After giving the young boy an earful, you send him on his way. Then you turn to the shopkeeper. You are furious! You had thought that this was a serious robbery, not merely a youngster's prank to steal a bar of candy. The cowardly shopkeeper has wasted your time. You may gain no Hero Points for this capture, but you must *lose* 1 Hero Point if you knocked out the young thief. In fact, if you did knock him out, you had better get moving quickly before any of the passers-by find out what has happened. This is just the sort of thing that your critics would pick up on. Will you leave quickly (turn to **438**), or would you like to give the shopkeeper a piece of your mind first (turn to **64**)?

317

The naval dockyard is a dismal place. In dock at the moment are three boats you can investigate: a small PT boat (turn to **417**), an ageing submarine (turn to **252**) and a battleship which is being painted (turn to **96**).

318

This has been a particularly savage murder. The man's throat has been slashed with a none-too-sharp blade. His wallet contains his business cards, which identify him as Wayne Bruce, President of Euro-American Security Inc. Also in his wallet is a photograph of an attractive blonde woman with dark eyes. One thing puzzles you. His wallet has not been touched! Certainly robbery was not the motive of this apparently normal mugging. Do you wish to head for the offices of Euro-American Security Inc. (turn to **233**), will you visit his home to talk to his wife (turn to **195**), or will you leave this crime in the hands of the police (turn to **73**)?

319

You had better avoid any more super exploits for a while. Do you want to pay a visit to your elderly aunt's house (turn to **134**), or will you go downtown to police headquarters to check that you are not required for any other duties (turn to **245**)?

320

Using *Energy Blast* will be dangerous, as a miss could cause the vial of poison to fall into the inlet. Will you risk it? If so, turn to **150**. If not, turn to **25**.

321

You approach the lion-tamer and exchange a few pleasantries. But while you keep up the conversation, you are also probing his mind for signs of any link between the attacks and the animals. But you cannot find any. If you wish to arrest the lion-tamer anyway, turn to **383**. If you leave the circus, turn to **148**.

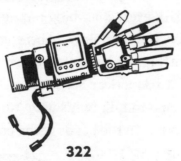

322

Evidently this is the theatre's most luxurious dressing-room, normally used by the stars. Elegant drapes line the walls, and a border of lights surrounds the mirror. But it is untouched. It looks as though it has not been used for weeks. There is nothing for you to find here. Will you try room number two (turn to **288**) or room number three (turn to **117**)?

323

The Chief Detective is contemptuous about super-heroes. In his eyes, fighting crime is a job for the police, not for what he calls 'amateur detectives'. Nevertheless, you do find some information about the event. The Alchemists, masters of advanced chemistry, had neutralized the alarm with some sort of acidic gas which delayed its being activated as they forced their way in. Another unknown compound had dissolved the security lock on the main door. Why the security guard had not noticed the intruders was still a mystery which would only be solved when the time-lock released him from the vault. But now he assures you that the situation is well under control in his hands. There is no need for any 'amateur in fancy pants' to get involved. Turn to **60**.

324

You emerge from the alley into a crowded street and look left and right. *Damn!* You cannot see him. You run a few paces along the street to search for any signs of him, but it is hopeless. He has escaped. Turn to **75**.

325

You have nothing you can use that will be especially effective against them. Turn to **78**.

326

You concentrate first on the creature's mind. Nothing happens. You are not sure that it even *has* one. Then you try a different approach. You will the water to heat. It starts to steam and the great creature feels the heat. It roars loudly and drops its victim into the fountain. The woman is unconscious and bleeding badly. You must return the water to normal temperature straight away. After doing this, you face the creature:

FOUNTAIN CREATURE *SKILL* 10 *STAMINA* 11

When you inflict your fourth hit on the creature, turn to **65**.

327

Next morning you leave for work early. You are sorely tempted to leave your Crimewatch behind; you dare not miss another day's work! But your fears are unwarranted. To your utter amazement, your Crimewatch is silent. You arrive at work early. Jonah Whyte cannot believe his eyes when he enters the office to find you hard at work at your desk. At lunch-time you catch up on the day's news on the teletext TV. Two stories catch your attention. One is of a strange attack in Audubon Park. A woman has been seriously mauled by what she calls 'a monster', but a specialist at the hospital thinks the claw-marks of an animal of some kind. The second story is of a man who had his chest crushed in the grounds of the Natural History Museum. There are no clues as to who or what was responsible. It is as if whatever caused the man's death simply walked away. Both incidents are being investigated by the police. You decide to do a little investigation of your own. You change into the Silver Crusader and set off to make your inquiries. Where will you head first:

The Natural History Museum?   Turn to **365**
Titan Zoo?   Turn to **408**
Warnum and Wailey's Travelling Circus? Turn to **4**

328

From your belt, you take a small rod the size of a pencil. It extends telescopically like a car aerial. This is a Radiation Neutralization Wand. In the battle that will follow, each time you score a hit, you have touched the dog with the wand and the effects of its radioactivity are neutralized. However, the dog can – and will – still fight, so you still have to defeat it. And if any dog bites a bystander, you will still lose a Hero Point, even if it has been touched with your wand. But a neutralized dog will not be able to kill you with a single attack unless this attack has reduced your *STAMINA* to zero. Turn to **237**.

You change trains and head for home. Are you wasting your time? After all, it's only a scrap of paper. How can you tell your boss that you were late for work because you wanted to check out a little piece of paper that you found in a cigarette packet? Nevertheless, you take it into your study, enter the words as they are written, and let your computer try to make some sense of them. Ten minutes later, it has printed three possible messages: 'Call the egg. You're wet behind the ears'; 'My newspaper is covered in plastic nodules'; and 'Idiot. Fear meeting address 176, not 178. Don't forget.' Interesting stuff. By now it is much too late to go to work. You spend the next hour working on a batch of phenolic acid. When it is ready you pour some in a vial and place it in your Accessory Belt to take with you. Will you now spend the rest of the day at the Wisneyland Amusement Park (turn to **15**), or will you go downtown, perhaps to do some shopping (turn to **202**)?

330

You aim an Energy Bolt at the tail of the plane as it rounds the corner on to the runway. But your aim is not accurate. The plane takes off into the sky. Turn to **249**.

331

Outside you find a single clue to the kidnapping – a metal slug with the letter M engraved in it. If this means anything to you, you will know how you can investigate it. Otherwise you have come to a dead end. You may give your information to the police and let them take over. Turn to **428**.

332

You draw a Micronet from your Accessory Belt and cast it over the creature. The tough fibres tangle its limbs, but it is not strong enough to hold for long. Turn to **373** to fight the Reincarnation, but deduct 3 points from its *SKILL* for the first six rounds of combat.

333

You pick up the piece of paper that he was trying to destroy. It bears the emblem of F.E.A.R.! The message is short: 'Do not forget. The meeting starts at 9 a.m.' Unfortunately, it bears no more information, but this time could be useful to you. You carry the Scarlet Prankster down to the ground and hand him over to the police. You may add 3 Hero Points for capturing him. Now turn to **103**.

334

You push past him and step into the back of the shop. He swats at you ineffectually from behind. You sweep aside a pair of curtains separating the front of the shop from the back. Four yellow faces look up at you from steamy washbowls. There seems to be nothing unusual here. Would you like to try Chomsky's upstairs (turn to **44**), or will you step back out to the street (turn to **368**)?

335

Although seemingly a harmless domestic servant, Vladimir Utoshski has made this particular Android specially to serve F.E.A.R. Apart from a 'Destruction' switch in its back which turns it into a creator of mayhem, it is armed with a deadly weapon – a poisonous dagger which it can make protrude from its right foot. A kick from this foot is certain death, a fact which you have just discovered. As the fast-acting poison takes effect, you can almost hear the leader of F.E.A.R. laughing. There is now nothing to prevent his meeting from taking place...

336

For capturing the Alchemists you may score 4 Hero Points. Such a waste, you think, that such brilliant minds should be used for criminal gain. If only they could be persuaded to devote themselves to academic research for the good of society. Turn now to **372**.

337

You spend a quiet evening reading a good book and have a hearty home-cooked meal. Add 6 *STAMINA* points and turn to **79**.

338

You rush out across the ice and begin hammering the surface around the girls with your fists. But it is no use; the ice is a metre thick. Head bowed, you must admit defeat. There is nothing you can do. The onlookers sneer at you as you leave the pool to try to phone someone who can help. You know what they must be thinking. What use have you been? You must lose 2 Hero Points for your failure. Then you can leave the pool by turning to **362**.

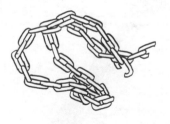

339

What will you do to prevent the bottle exploding? Will you throw it out of the window (turn to **269**), smother it with your hands (turn to **426**), or rush off to look for a fire-extinguisher (turn to **89**)?

A fire has started in the rear of the car

340

You take your vial of phenolic acid and hurl it at the creature. Roll two dice and compare the total with your *SKILL* score. If you roll a number *higher than* your *SKILL,* you have missed and you will have to take on the Devastator with your bare hands (turn to **262**). If the roll is *equal to or less than* your *SKILL,* turn to **69**.

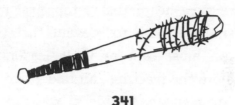

341

Late again... You creep past the office of your boss, Jonah Whyte, hoping he will not notice. But no such luck. His voice booms out at you: 'Lafayette! In my office. *Immediately!'* Sheepishly, you leave your desk and creep in to see him. A stream of abuse follows. In his eyes you are lazy, shiftless, incompetent... Suddenly a squeal of tyres in the street below, followed by a loud crash, interrupts him and the two of you rush to the window. A crowd is gathering around a large black limousine which has spun round in the road, mounted the sidewalk and crashed into a street-lamp. A fire has started in the rear of the car and is spreading. Do you wish to run downstairs in your street clothes (turn to **102**), or nip into the toilet to change into the Silver Crusader (turn to **23**)? Alternatively you may ignore the incident and go back to work (turn to **167**).

342

You arrive at the army base and are escorted to see Colonel Saunders, who greets you with a warm handshake. 'Crusader!' he smiles. 'Well, this is an honour. What can we do for you?' You explain you have come to compare notes on the activities of F.E.A.R. 'So far,' Saunders starts, 'we have come up with nothing. Like you, we have heard that a top-level meeting is imminent and if we are to prevent their villainous escapades, we must capture their leader, Vladimir Utoshski, before the meeting can take place. They are powerful, Crusader, and ruthless. You can count on all the help we can give you.' Suddenly an aide bursts into the room. 'Sir!' he pants. 'Helicopters! Identity unknown! Coming towards the base at four o'clock!' The Colonel leaps into action. 'Contact them on the radio. If they will not identify themselves, we will open fire.' If you have *Super Strength,* you fly out to investigate (turn to **379**). Otherwise, turn to **58**.

343

All is quiet at the reactor, apart from endless tramping of the numerous armed security guards who have been positioned to guard it. There is no sign of Knox. You wait for half an hour, but still nothing happens. Suddenly a klaxon sounds and men and women rush to their positions. The cooling-system, which was checked thoroughly an hour ago, is malfunctioning. The reactor is overloading! You rush round to the other side of the reactor and, in front of you, you see the cause. Sidney Knox, his head bloated like a pumpkin, is staring at the structure. Guards are aiming their weapons at him, but no one has given the order to fire. They breathe a sigh of relief when they see you, and look to you for guidance. If you have *Super Strength,* turn to **33**. If you have *Energy Blast,* turn to **204**. If you have *Psi-Powers,* turn to **419**. If you have *ETS,* turn to **80**.

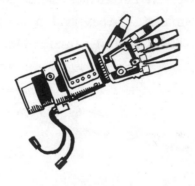

344

You send a carefully charged Energy Bolt in the direction of the boxes. It strikes the bottom box (there is no need to test for aim) and the whole pile topples over backwards on top of the thief. A shrill scream comes from the villain. The foot twitches and then rests motionless. You step over cautiously to investigate. Turn to **286**.

345

The dinosaur exhibits are very realistic, but the curator merely laughs when you suggest the possibility of one of them being responsible for the man's death. 'Apart from the fact that these creatures have been dead for several million years,' he chuckles, 'how on earth would you suggest they got out of the building? Through the doors? One of these brutes would take the side of the museum with it if it decided to go and look for another home! No, if you're looking for clues to the murder, I suggest you try Titan zoo. You'll have better luck there.' You feel a little foolish for even making the suggestion. If you want to try the zoo, turn to **408**. Otherwise turn to **148**.

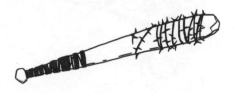

346

While the struggle is fought, the aircraft falls into a steep dive. Your last blow fells your foe. As he slumps to the floor, you grab the controls of the plummeting aircraft and shout for the stewardess. She arrives and is able to untie the pilots. In the nick of time they take over from you and are able to guide the plane down to a safe landing. Turn to **35**.

347

The heating engineer shows you round the plant. He is mystified as to what happened; there is nothing wrong with the heating-equipment. You double-check the controls and scratch your head. Nothing wrong there. Perhaps no one will ever know what caused the incident, but at least the danger is now over. Turn to **362**.

348

Your powers reveal that she is telling the truth. The murderer will remain a mystery. Turn to **73**.

349

Everything is normal at the airport as you arrive. You do not want to cause any panic, so you change into your street clothes and proceed with your plan. You may head for one of the three hangars to look for clues. Xavier Hangar is where private and executive jets are kept. Summers Hangar houses emergency helicopters. McCoy Hangar is for cargo aircraft. Which will you investigate:

Xavier Hangar?	Turn to **394**
Summers Hangar?	Turn to **46**
McCoy Hangar?	Turn to **115**

350

You are congratulated by the crowd for having averted what could have been a disaster. Note the Hero Points that you have scored, deducting 1 point from the original 4 for each bystander that was bitten by a dog. As you leave the University, a crowd of autograph hunters has gathered outside. Will you slip out the back way to avoid them and make for home (turn to **293**), or oblige by stepping out to face the crowd (turn to **397**)?

351

You change into your street clothes and sit down in the diner, hoping to notice something suspicious. An hour, and several cups of coffee, later, a group of shifty-looking characters enter and sit down at a table. Turn to **302**.

352

You will need two Energy Bolts to stop the creature. If you do not wish to risk using two Bolts, turn to **373** to finish off the fight hand to hand. If your first Bolt was a hit, you may reduce its *STAMINA* by 6 points. Turn to **239** if you win.

353

You rush off to find police officers or stadium officials who might be able to help you. Your first priority must be to organize an evacuation of the west stand. But your plans are futile, as you realize when you hear a great crashing coming from behind you. The stand is down! The Creature of Carnage stands in the centre of the wreckage, roaring loudly. People, dead and dying, surround him. He turns to go and there is nothing you can do to stop him. Your first duty is to aid the injured people around him. When you have done what you can, turn to **40**.

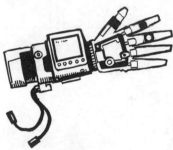

354

Luckily, the other two are not armed with chemical weapons. Fight them one at a time:

	SKILL	STAMINA
Second ALCHEMIST	7	7
Third ALCHEMIST	7	6

If you defeat them, turn to **336**.

Four flaming bodies stomp around the shop

There must be something he'd like. No doubt he's already got Monopoly. What about this: Trivial Pursuit? Looks interesting. Or how about Dungeons & Dragons? Hmm. He probably hasn't got the imagination. As you are perusing the games, four bikers walk in in ripped jeans and dirty leather jackets. Trouble. You watch them from the corner of your eye. They are in the women's underwear department and are holding bras up to their chests and laughing. A middle-aged woman comes over to stop them and an assistant manager steps in to help. Tempers rise. Just when you are wondering whether or not to join in, one of the bikers throws his jacket to the floor. He clasps his hands together and to the horror of the unsuspecting floor staff, he bursts into flames! The others do likewise and four flaming bodies stomp about the shop, setting fire to everything they touch. The Fire Warriors! Of course! Why did you not recognize those no-good delinquents earlier? You had better act quickly. If you have *Super Strength,* turn to **133**. If you have *Psi-Powers,* turn to **178**. If you have *ETS,* turn to **156**. If you have *Energy Blast,* turn to **283**.

356

You emerge from the alley into a crowded street and look left and right. *Damn!* You cannot see him. You run a few paces along the street to search for any signs of him, but it is hopeless. He has escaped. Turn to **75**.

357

To the beat of loud disco music, cars are circling round the track bashing into one another and causing hoots of laughter for their drivers. Your own car, Blue 7, seems to be a little slower than the rest, but you nevertheless get a couple of satisfying head-ons before your eyes catch sight of the danger... A young boy driving Red 14 is smashed in the side by Yellow 3. The collision knocks him sideways and out of his car on to the metal mat of the track in front of you. The driver of Purple 10, who was just lining up a head-on collision with you, screams and throws her hands up in the air as she sees the danger. The boy is lying right between your two cars! How quick are your reactions? Can you avert the collision about to crush the boy? Roll two dice and compare the total with your *SKILL* score. If the total *exceeds* your *SKILL,* turn to **388**. Otherwise turn to **234**.

358

The exhausted mutant falls to his knees. Though you too have been tired by the strain, you have not finished yet. By sheer force of mind, you will him to repair the leaks to the system. One by one the leaks begin to close. Eventually the klaxon stops sounding. The danger is over! You may gain 2 Hero Points for your success. In appreciation of your saving the Laboratory, the scientists bring you a small pen-like device. 'Crusader, take this as a gift from us,' pleads the Institute Director. 'One of our men made it in his spare time. He calls it a "Circuit Jammer". It is still to be fully tested, but seems to work okay. I know you often face mechanical villains and their contraptions. With this, you will be able to disable their circuits. You are looking for Vladimir Utoshski and he is a powerful adversary. With this you will stand a better chance.' You thank the Director for his gift. It may well come in handy. Now turn to **125**.

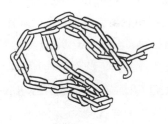

359

You temporarily release your grip on him and he manages to shove you aside, just as the President's car draws past. He aims the gun and shoots! The President falls! You leap on him again to finish off the battle (he was *SKILL* 7, *STAMINA* 6). If you defeat him, turn to **374**.

360

You crouch down underneath the lion cage. Sure enough, at the far end is a trapdoor leading up to one end of the cage, into an area which appears to be the lions' shelter. You listen at the trapdoor and can hear shuffling sounds coming from within. Every so often a man's voice chuckles. You shove the trapdoor up and leap inside. Standing in a small room is a sharp-featured man with a long waxed moustache. He is dressed in a bright red suit with a large top hat – the Ringmaster! Surrounding him, pinned to the walls, are photographs of twelve people and several have black lines drawn across them. You recognize photographs of the woman savaged by 'a monster' and the man crushed in the grounds of the Natural History Museum. Twelve people? Of course! The jury which condemned the Ringmaster to fifteen years in prison! He leaps to his feet as you burst in and you will have to fight him:

THE RINGMASTER   *SKILL* 8   *STAMINA* 6

After the first round of combat, turn to **207**.

361

You arrive at Cowfield Dairy and make a thorough inspection of their sterilization equipment. The staff are most co-operative and are as anxious to find out what happened as you are. All seems to be in order and there is no clue as to how the Poisoner managed to drop traces of his poison into the two milk-bottles. You have no way of pursuing this case further. Turn to **107**.

362

Where will you go next? Perhaps you deserve a little entertainment. The Titan Tigers, a local football team, are playing the Metro Mohawks. If you want to go and watch the game, turn to **114**. If you are more concerned about finding information about the activities of F.E.A.R., you may wish to visit Colonel Saunders at his army base to see whether he knows anything (turn to **342**).

363

Fire an Energy Bolt at the creature. When you first hit it, turn to **48**.

364

You grab Karpov and threaten to finish him off unless he tells you what he knows about F.E.A.R. The man cringes and agrees, but pleads with you that he doesn't know much. A meeting is taking place tomorrow at 11 a.m., but he does not know where the meeting will be, as he has not been invited. You hand the villain over to the police. You may add 5 Hero Points for defeating him. Turn to **40**.

365

The curator of the Natural History Museum is very helpful and agrees to show you round the exhibits. Will you ask him to show you the model reconstructions of dinosaurs (turn to **345**) or the 'large mammals' section (turn to **253**)?

366

If you have *ETS,* turn to **205**. If you have *Super Strength,* turn to **137**. Otherwise turn to **267**.

367

Take aim and fire your *Energy Blast*. The first hit will cause the poor girl gripped in its jaws to be released. Another will be necessary to kill the creature. When you have inflicted a second hit, turn to **265**.

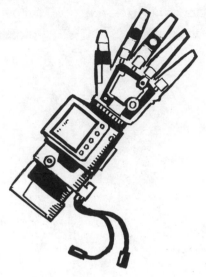

368

It is hopeless. You do not know where F.E.A.R. is holding its meeting and you have no chance of finding it in such a short time. You find a convenient spot, change into your street clothes and hail a cab. The driver has his radio on. As he chats away, the radio splutters and fizzles. The music dies and an unscheduled announcement interrupts the programme. Turn to **292**.

Your eye catches a familiar-looking figure

369

You change in a convenient alley and head for the Dairy. When you arrive at the gates, everything seems to be in order. Milk-floats are returning from their daily rounds and thousands of bottles are chinking their way along conveyors. There is no sign of danger. A short-tailed tabby cat – no doubt a stray – is trying to get in through the gates. You pick the hungry creature up and stroke it. As you wait, your eye catches a familiar-looking figure turning the corner and walking towards you. It is 'Chain-saw' Bronski, a well-known murderer who you thought was well behind bars! Will you apprehend the villain (turn to **3**), or does your first duty lie with the needy and will you instead take the cat to a Cats' Home (turn to **278**)?

370

It is a fine day and the Marina is bustling with activity. Tomorrow is the annual Titan City Regatta and many of the wealthy yacht owners are entering their boats. This does not help you in your search for clues leading to the whereabouts of the F.E.A.R. meeting. You comb the Marina until you finally find a salty old fisherman who is mending his net. If you wish to talk to him, turn to **221**. Otherwise turn to **368**.

371

There are three of them against one of you. But the two knuckle-faced bodyguards begin to panic. 'B-b-boss! That there's the Silver Crusader! We don' want no tangles with no superheroes! That mother's mean. We ain't got nothin' to save us from an Energy Bolt!' The three of them give up without a fight. You have earned 3 Hero Points. Now turn to **73**.

372

Where will your next mission take you? Remembering the police officer's plea and the Crimewatch's message, you may either head for the beach (turn to **72**) or Parker Airport (turn to **410**).

373

The Reincarnation is a powerful creature which may not be killed. But you may be able to knock it unconscious; if you reduce its *STAMINA* to zero, it will remain so for two days. Resolve the battle:

THE REINCARNATION   SKILL 10   STAMINA 12

If you defeat the creature, turn to **239**.

374

You haul the unconscious assassin out of the crowd towards the President's car. Swarms of police are surrounding the car and, in the distance, you can hear an ambulance's siren approaching. One of the President's bodyguards is listening for a pulse. He looks up and shakes his head. In your street clothes, you cannot get near the body, but the police listen to your story and take the assassin from you. One of them talks to another, who talks to another standing in the car. They seem to be considering your story. Word gets back to you: 'Something strange is going on. You say this guy fired at the President as he fell? Then how come the bullet that killed him came from a high-powered rifle, not the Magnum your man was carrying?' You are as mystified as they are and agree to go downtown to answer their questions. But one thing is clear. Your assassin's bullet did not kill the President. Was he merely a decoy? You puzzle over this as you leave the station and head for home. Turn to **311**.

375

As luck would have it, you manage to keep all the dogs from escaping out into the corridor. They now stand facing you, snarling menacingly. Turn to **120**.

376

While you struggle, the plane has entered a steep dive. With the madman shrieking with insane glee, you try desperately to subdue him in time to prevent a disaster. But to no avail. The Tormentor is too powerful. Before you can get to the controls, the plane hurtles down to the runway and explodes, killing all on board...

377

There is no sign of Knox anywhere around the test laboratories, but one scientist believes he saw a man fitting his description jump into a car and drive away from the Lab towards town. Do you want to follow this lead back into Titan City (turn to **254**), or will you instead try the nuclear reactor (turn to **343**)?

378

You fly up in front of the Devastator and land a heavy blow in its chest. The creature groans and turns to face you:

THE DEVASTATOR   *SKILL 14*   *STAMINA 12*

If you defeat it, turn to **119**.

379

You fly out over the camp fence towards the advancing helicopters. Some twenty helicopters are flying low in towards the camp. You stop in mid-air as you see the insignia on the side of the leader. It is the death's head of F.E.A.R.! As it flies closer, you can see who is leading this attack. The Macro Brain! A product of genetic experimentation, like yourself, the Macro Brain has developed a tremendous intelligence. But unlike yourself, he has decided to use it to further the cause of evil. A formidable combination, you think. On your own there is little you could do against twenty choppers. But perhaps you could take out the leading one carrying your old foe... As you consider this, a warning comes from your Crimewatch. *'COUNCIL BUILDINGS, FAST.'* You consider your options. Will you decide to attack the leading helicopter to try to defeat the mastermind behind this attack (turn to **32**), or will you leave this matter to the army and head into town to find out what is happening at Titan Council Buildings (turn to **154**)?

380

You bind the Fire Warriors with rope and help the staff clear the damage until the police arrive. You may claim as many Hero Points as the number of Fire Warriors you captured. Then you had better change back to Jean Lafayette and make your way to work. If you want to run to work, turn to **301**. If you feel it would be quicker to take the subway train, turn to **409**.

'He's going to poison the water supply!'

381

The little man disappears into the back room. Five minutes later, he reappears with a tray. On the tray is your Peking Duck! He is most put out when you refuse to pay for the food. This is getting you nowhere. You leave the laundry. Turn to **368**.

382

You remember your clue and follow its advice. When you arrive at the reservoir, you are surprised to find the office door unlocked. Inside, you find the reason why. The on-duty clerk is lying in a corner of the office, bound and gagged. You untie his hands and take the gag from his mouth. 'Crusader!' he whispers. 'Thank goodness you're here! But forget about me. You've got to get into the pump-house fast. It's the Poisoner. He's going to poison the water-supply! Quickly!' You rush to the pump-house and fling back the door. A wild-haired man is leaning over a network of pipes, studying the valves. In his hand he holds a vial of liquid. As you enter, he wheels round. An evil grin greets you. 'The Silver Crusader, eh?' he laughs. 'So you think you can foil my plan. Well, hold your ground. See this vial? One step closer and I'll pour it into this intake and within an hour my poison will be flowing out of the taps of every household in Titan City!' You must stop the Poisoner before he can carry out his plan. If you have *Energy Blast,* turn to **320**. If you have *Psi-Powers,* turn to **81**. If you have *Super Strength,* turn to **25**. If you have *ETS,* turn to **235**.

383

You arrest the lion-tamer and take him down to police headquarters. The man is incredulous and protests his innocence all the way. When you arrive at headquarters, the desk sergeant wants to know what charges you are bringing against the lion-tamer. When you can offer no evidence at all as proof of his guilt, the sergeant shakes his head. The lion-tamer must be released. Calling you all the names under the sun, he leaves the station. You must lose 2 Hero Points for this wrongful arrest. Turn now to **148**.

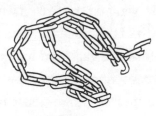

384

You concentrate hard on the creature's mind. It stops for a moment, shakes its head and looks at you. Are you getting through to it? You believe you are, and you step forward to increase your influence. This is a fatal mistake. For as you step forward, the Creature of Carnage snaps out of its trance and swats at you. You are knocked off your feet and your head cracks against a girder. You lose consciousness and you never see the results of the Creature's devastation. For it succeeds in bringing the whole stand down, killing hundreds of people – and you are among the dead...

385

You rush to the idol and check for the ear-rings. There are none there! The professor thumbs through the catalogue to double-check the idol. 'Er, ahem!' he snorts. 'Ah, my mistake, Crusader. This idol does not have ear-rings at all. My, my. I am getting very forgetful in my old age...' A false alarm. Looks like all is well, after all. You decide not to waste any further time here, and you leave. Turn to **276**.

386

In the personal column of the newspaper you find an interesting snippet, which reads: 'Richard Storm. All is forgiven. How was I to know she was a private nurse? Phone me on 555–9999. Love, Susan.' A private nurse? What is this all about? If you now want to proceed to the bank as the Silver Crusader, turn to **112**. If you want to go to work, turn to **341**.

387

You race after Utoshski through the milling crowds and catch a glimpse of him leaving the exhibition through a fire-door. You follow him into an alley. He is nowhere to be seen! He must have run to one end of the alley into the street. Will you try turning left (turn to **356**) or right (turn to **324**)?

388

It is hopeless. Your car is too slow to react. The two cars collide, not with each other, but into the young boy on the ground. The ride stops immediately as the boy's mother rushes on to the track shrieking. Five minutes later an ambulance arrives to rush the boy to hospital. But it is too late; he has died. Feeling ashamed that you could do nothing to help the boy, you leave. You have had enough of Wisneyland for the day. Turn to **103**.

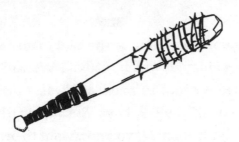

389

You concentrate hard on the ice around the two swimmers. A puddle of water appears around them and their spirits rise. You are melting the ice! But the mental effort you are using is considerable. You must lose 4 *STAMINA* points to free the two girls, but when you have done so, you may add 2 Hero Points for undoubtedly saving their lives. You will not be able to melt the whole pool; you will have to leave this to time. You may leave by turning to **362**. If you wish, you may check the pool heating-plant before you leave, by turning to **347**.

390

You try to smash the door. It shakes, but there is nothing you can do. It is made of ten-centimetre solid metal. Even your great strength cannot break it. You try again, but without success. However, your attempts to smash the door do attract the attentions of the crew. *'An intruder!'* cries someone. 'Locked in the ejection chamber!' You can guess what they will do next. A rumbling sound from the walls around you is followed by a loud hissing. Next thing you know you are forcibly fired out of the submarine into the sea. The shock is too much for you. You pass out, never to regain consciousness. It doesn't take long for your lungs to fill with water. . .

391

You arrive at a disused warehouse in the industrial district. The door is open and you can hear voices coming from upstairs. Will you creep slowly up the stairs, ready for action (turn to **277**), or will you get up on the roof and swing through the window to surprise them (turn to **396**)?

392

You follow the Macro Brain into the Colonel's study and wait for the right moment to use *Energy Blast*. As you are about to send a Bolt, your opponent wheels round to face you. 'Crusader!' he laughs. 'So you have joined the army, eh? Well let's see if we can persuade you to join *my* army.' You try to fire your Bolt. Nothing happens! The tremendous mental powers of the Macro Brain have interfered with your own special abilities. Seconds later, you feel a sharp stabbing pain in your chest. Your old foe has developed much more far-reaching mental powers then he ever had before. You are powerless to prevent him sapping the energy from you! You fall to your knees in submission, but still he will not relent. For the Macro Brain will not stop until you have been reduced to a virtual mindless zombie. Your career as a superhero is over. . .

393

The crowd love you. You sign autographs for ten minutes and kiss a couple of babies, then make your excuses and leave. Jonah Whyte will *be furious* when you arrive at work. But your public-spirited attitude has been good for PR. Add 1 Hero Point and head for work. Turn to **435**.

394

When you arrive in Xavier Hangar, mechanics are servicing two executive jets. You find a pair of overalls hanging on the wall, slip into them and wander around. There is nothing suspicious. In fact you are not expecting anything to happen for a couple of hours. What time of day are you expecting the meeting to take place? Add this time to today's date and add the result to this reference. If the resulting reference makes no sense, turn to **220**.

395

An obliging attendant is happy to show you the body of the mysterious man. He looks up a file and reaches for the handle on a cadaver drawer. His eyes open wide as he pulls the drawer out. It is empty! He double-checks the number and shakes his head. 'I can't understand it!' he says. 'I put him in here myself! And I've been here all the time except for . . . my coffee break.' The trail ends here. There are no clues as to the whereabouts of the missing body. You can leave the hospital by turning to **226**.

396

You time your swing perfectly. The Mantrapper and two henchmen are sitting just inside, with Drew Swain tied up on a chair nearby. Smashing through the glass, you land in the centre of the group, your feet catching both henchmen. One topples over backwards and rolls into a self-locking cage, which slams shut, trapping him inside. The other rolls over to the stairwell and crashes through the bannister to land with a thud at the bottom of the stairs. Now it's just you against the Mantrapper:

MANTRAPPER   *SKILL 8*   *STAMINA 7*

If you defeat him, turn to **16**.

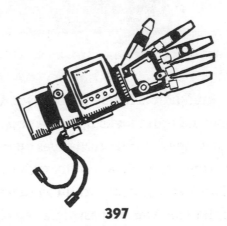

397

The crowd cheers as you walk down the steps of the building. You are surrounded by energetic hands thrusting pieces of paper at you. You have signed a dozen or so autographs when your ears prick up. A cry is coming from a shop a few doors down: 'Stop! *Thief!*' Sounds like a job for the Silver Crusader! You break through the crowd to investigate. Turn to **256**.

Under the watchful eye of your boss, you complete the morning's work. At lunch-time, you take a corner booth at El Greco's, a cheap diner on the next block. While you are eating, a chattering group of boffin-types scramble into the booth next to yours. They are trying to keep their voices down, but their obvious excitement allows you to catch the gist of their conversation. They are from the local university's science laboratory. 'Well, I think the man's a fool!' says one. 'If he mixes the aldehyde in at *that* temperature there could be an almighty explosion.' 'Maybe you're right,' says another. 'He's a stubborn old jackass. He'd never admit it was dangerous. I know one thing; we're much safer out here!' Hmmm, you think. Sounds ominous. Perhaps you'd better check it out. The group's security-passes identify them as being from the Biochemistry Department – only a block away. You pay your bill and leave quickly. Halfway there, you stop. From within the shop you are passing, a cry reaches you. 'Stop! *Thief!*' Will you investigate this call for help (turn to **256**), or do you think stopping a potential explosion is a much more important task (turn to **144**)?

399

Honking furiously, he pulls you round to the far side of the circus towards a large, brightly coloured caravan. You walk up the steps and open the door. 'Good afternoon, good afternoon!' says a plump lady behind a desk inside. 'We have only a few seats left for tonight's performance, but I'm sure we can find you something suitable. How many tickets do you want?' You explain that you have not come for tickets. Will you ask her where you can find the owner of the circus and follow her directions (turn to **223**), or will you ask her whether she knows anything about any escaped animals (turn to **291**)?

400

The Bolt catches the assassin in the back. He howls and throws up his hands, losing his grip on the rifle, which drops from the roof. The shock has made him lose his balance and he slumps forward, over the edge of the roof! You rush to the edge just in time to see him land in the crowd below, no doubt causing some considerable injuries to the onlookers. You have saved the President's life, but have also caused a serious accident. Add 1 Hero Point and turn to **311**.

401

One of the dogs has not been fully subdued! It breaks past

you through the door and rushes into the crowd, growling menacingly. You must pursue it immediately before it can harm anyone:

RADIATION DOG   SKILL 7   STAMINA 5

If it rolls a higher Attack Strength than your own, turn to **31**, *but first note this reference, as you will have to return here afterwards.* If you defeat the dog, turn to **247**.

402

You pull a small metal gadget from your Accessory Belt and aim it at the boxes. Your Forcefield Generator hums; the boxes sway, topple over and fall on the thief. There is a shrill scream. The protruding foot shakes and then rests still. Cautiously, you walk over to investigate. Turn to **286**.

403

The study is not empty. As you enter, a figure stands over the desk, leafing through a notebook and taking pictures with a radio camera! The maid screams at the sight of the Smoke, an ethereal villain who is able to turn himself at will into a vapour. As you enter he drops the camera and smiles. Turning himself into a whisk of brown smoke, he streaks across the room and disappears through the air-conditioner. You race outside the house. Turn to **29**.

404

You have no special gadgets you can use against such a creature, the likes of which you have never seen before. You will have to fight it:

FOUNTAIN CREATURE   *SKILL 10*   *STAMINA 11*

Your first hit will cause it to drop the injured girl into the fountain. When you have inflicted your fourth hit, turn to **65**.

405

You reach into a thorny bush and your fingers touch a metallic object. Grasping it as best you can, you pull out a gold medallion hanging on a delicate chain. As you turn it over in your hand, you realize it is undoubtedly quite valuable. The medallion has the initials D.R. engraved on it. Will you hand this over to the police (turn to **251**), or take it to a jeweller (turn to **17**)? Alternatively you may wish to visit another address. If so, add together the number and street number of this address and turn to this reference.

406

The Alchemists emerge, and you turn on your Sonic Confuser. In front of you, the gang raise their hands to their ears and scream with pain. But around them, pedestrians, including two young girls, are doing the same. You cannot risk harming the public. You fiddle with the gadget to turn it off, but already the gang have turned the corner and escaped. You have lost them! Turn to **372**.

<h2 style="text-align:center">407</h2>

Test your Luck. If you are Lucky, turn to **196**. If you are Unlucky, turn to **56**.

<h2 style="text-align:center">408</h2>

When you arrive at the zoo gates, you question the attendant, asking whether there have been any reports of animals escaping from their cages over the last couple of days. The attendant is obviously excited to see you. 'Gosh. Hi, Crusader!' he stammers. 'Er, yes. I did hear something about an escape. But I don't know any more about it. You'll have to ask the Director. I'll take you to him if you like.' You tell him to lead the way. But as you turn to follow him, a *beep – beep – beep* comes from your wrist. You hold the Crimewatch up to your ear. *'MUSEUM OF EGYPTIAN HERITAGE,'* it speaks. Do you want to follow its advice and head straight away for the museum (turn to **158**), or will you ignore this message and instead follow the attendant (turn to **26**)?

409

The office is only two stops away. Surprisingly, you don't have to wait long for a train to arrive. You sit and contemplate a good excuse to give to Mr Whyte, who is bound to be in a foul mood when you arrive, but a cry interrupts your thoughts. *'Help!'* you hear, from a voice at the other end of the carriage. Oh, no! What is it this time? As if in answer, the voice cries: *'PICKPOCKET!'* You had better see if you can help – but there will be no opportunity to change into the Silver Crusader. Will you go and help the man (turn to **185**), or will you ignore him and concern yourself with getting to work on time for once (turn to **301**)?

410

You arrive at Parker Airport and ask the nearest security guard whether anything is happening. 'The Silver Crusader!' he gasps. 'Thank goodness you're here! Follow me. I'll take you to the Control Tower.' You follow him up into the Control Tower where you find the place buzzing with activity. The Air-Traffic Controller greets you nervously. 'Have you heard? No? The police are on their way. Some guy calling himself "the Tormentor" has hijacked a DC10 full of passengers to London. He's mad! No demands; nothing. Says he'll crash the plane. Blames it all on "Susan". We don't know what to do. A complete nutter! Is there anything you can do?' Is there anything you can do? If 'Susan' means anything to you, turn to **141**. If not, you can use your powers. If you have *Super Strength,* turn to **84**. If you have *Psi-Powers,* turn to **216**. Otherwise, turn to **176**.

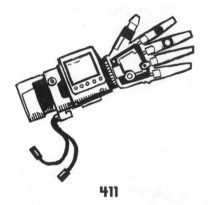

411

You press the button on your Circuit Jammer. The Cyborg's grin fades as the device affects its electronic functions. Its abilities have been reduced to those of an ordinary man! Now you may battle the villain on more equal terms:

TITANIUM CYBORG   *SKILL 9*   *STAMINA 10*

If you defeat the villain, turn to **19**.

412

You arrive at police headquarters and speak to Lieutenant Wojak, who seems to be quite distressed. "The news has leaked out, Crusader,' he explains. 'We were trying to keep the Poisoner's threats a secret, but it seems some reporter got his hands on the story. The Poisoner has asked for a million in unmarked notes by this evening, otherwise he says everyone in Titan City will suffer. You know the guy: he's a madman. *And* he's involved with that F.E.A.R. organization. What can we do?' Apparently two citizens have already died from minute traces of poison found in their milk-bottles. You offer to try to track him down. Where will you begin your search? The Cowfield Dairy (turn to **361**), or the city's largest drug store in Schuter Mall (turn to **268**)? If there is somewhere else you'd like to go, you will know how to get there.

413

You have no time to concentrate; she attacks straight away. Resolve this combat:

TIGER CAT   *SKILL 9*   *STAMINA 8*

If you win, turn to **217**.

414

You leap into the air and shoot after the van. Half a kilometre ahead, you see it about to make a turn. You drop down in front of it, forcing it to stop. The driver stares. 'Say,' he greets you. 'Ain't you that Crusader cat? Well, I sure am glad to meet you. Yesiree.' You tell him you are going to take a look in the back of his van and step round to the back. He follows you, still jabbering. 'But why, Crusader baby? Ain't nothin' in there but a coupl'a porkies, a coupl'a chicken...' You open the door and are greeted with a blast which knocks you three metres backwards, to land in a lifeless heap in the road!' 'Oh yeah, nearly forgot,' chuckles the man, 'an' a laser cannon. That ol' Mantrapper sure do have things worked out well. Yes indeed.' You have fallen right into a cleverly executed trap. The van was merely a decoy. And a deadly one at that: your mistake has cost you your life...

415

Quick as a flash, you reach forward and grab the girl in the nick of time before she plunges to certain death. Her parents are horrified at the dreadful accident which might have occurred. When the ride is over, they thank you profusely for saving their daughter's life. You decide that you have had enough of Wisneyland. Turn to **103**.

416

He studies the closed-circuit security screens which are focused on the main treasures of his collection. Everything seems to be in order. But he does study one screen rather closely. It is a figurehead of the god Amon-Ra, festooned with golden jewellery. He is not sure whether there is supposed to be a pair of golden ear-rings on the idol. Do you want to go and check it (turn to **385**), or will you instead check the main exhibit, the sarcophagus of Princess Ankalis (turn to **240**)?

417

There is nothing particularly suspicious about the boat. Indeed it would be a most unsuitable place to have a meeting, since there is no room for anyone apart from the crew on board. Turn to **368**.

418

From your Accessory Belt you draw out your Directional Sound Neutralizer. Focusing it on the noisy crowd, you send a charge into the centre. Its effect is immediate. By neutralizing all the sound-waves within range of its effect, no one can hear what anyone else is saying! Baffled by their apparent deafness, the crowd turn towards you. You turn off the Sound Neutralizer. Voices whisper: 'The Silver Crusader!' In a booming voice you command them to cease their squabbling and disperse.

They do as you say. Now you must change back into your street clothes and choose your next move. Will you continue your original journey to work (turn to **341**), or head into Audubon Park (turn to **165**)?

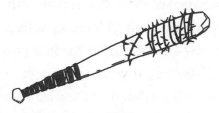

419

You concentrate hard on the immensely powerful mind within Sidney Knox's body. You must resolve the following combat as if it were a normal fight, but in this case, it represents a mind-to-mind battle between Knox's will and your own. While fighting this one out, your *SKILL* is the same as your current *SKILL* score, and your 'mental' *STAMINA* is 6 (you will not lose any 'real' *STAMINA* points).

SIDNEY KNOX   *SKILL 7*   *STAMINA 6*

Each time you lose a round of combat, the effect on your physical body wears down your *SKILL*. *YOU* must permanently lose 1 *SKILL* point for each Attack Round which you lose. If you defeat him, turn to **358**. If you wish to break mental combat, you will have to attack him physically (turn to **33**).

420

The Manager, Roger Stevens, wants to do all he can to help. He was woken in the early morning by a call from the police. The Alchemists, masters of advanced chemistry, had neutralized the alarm with some sort of acidic gas which delayed its being activated as they forced their way in. Another unknown compound had dissolved the security lock on the main door. Why the security guard had not noticed the intruders was still a mystery which would only be solved when the time-lock released him from the vault. You ask him about his deposit-box holders and he becomes less co-operative. Some of the boxes are owned by important citizens, and their identities must not be disclosed. Will you try to find out more about the deposit-box owners (turn to **83**), or question the Chief Detective (turn to **323**) or the security guard (turn to **259**)?

421

Using a Spectral Analyser, you are surprised to discover that the police chief's guess was probably not far from the truth. The creature seems to be made of a sort of rock. The nearest equivalent is the kind of substance found in fallen meteors! But how will you attempt to defeat it? If you have a vial of phenolic acid, turn to **340**. If you want to try to take it on with your bare hands, turn to **262**. If you feel this creature is a little too strong for you, turn to **319**.

422

You concentrate on the creature's mind, but you are unable to get through to it. In fact you are unsure whether it has a mind at all, or whether it is motivated simply by instinct. You try a different tack. Running round the side of the empty grave, you watch the creature carefully as it follows you. As it steps forwards, you *will* the ground to open up under its foot. A crack appears on the ground and when the Reincarnation's foot touches the soil, it drops a metre into the grave! The jolt has injured it, but certainly has not stopped it. You must now turn to **373** to fight it, but deduct 4 *STAMINA* points from its score, for the fall it has just had.

423

You study the cigarette packet. It is an ordinary packet of Karlsboroughs, but contains no cigarettes. The piece of paper inside makes no sense at all; a few meaningless words strung together. Is it really meaningless, or perhaps some kind of code? If it is a code, it means nothing to you. If you have *ETS,* you could take it home and run it through your Decoding Computer (turn to **329**). But this will take some time, and you ought to be getting to work. Otherwise you can save it, and give it some thought later (turn to **86**).

Screams break out and the Android goes beserk

424

You spend half an hour winding round the stacked shelves of the supermarket, choosing what you will be eating over the next couple of days. Eventually you pay for your groceries and leave. Turn to **226**.

425

The crowds are gathering to get into the exhibition, and a huge banner proclaims: *'APPLIANCES OF THE FUTURE* – See Tomorrow's Home Technology Today!' As you wander through the exhibitions, there are many excited voices enthusing over the more ambitious gadgets on show. The 'Clothing Service Station', for example, is a machine which takes in dirty washing and cleans, dries and irons it, ready to wear. A 'Cocktail Composer' puts together all the ingredients of a cocktail. 'The Perfect Opponent' is a games-playing computer which can learn the rules of any game and will play at eight different levels of skill. Robots are there in many forms. A 'Tidy Maid' remembers where everything goes in a room and will replace everything in its proper position. On a large stand, a man with round glasses and a loud voice is demonstrating his firm's 'Tireless Butler', a man-sized Android which will do many home chores. You stare at him. His face looks familiar, but you can't quite place him. The Android passes him a cigarette as he is bending down, but catches his hair and moves it slightly. A wig! Of course! With a bald head, his identity is obvious. Although he is not easy to recognize without the cybernetic enhancers he wears on his arms and his distinctive – and very dangerous – eye-goggles, it most certainly is Vladimir Utoshski, head of F.E.A.R.! You quickly nip away to change into the Silver Crusader, and return to capture the villain. But he is quick. He sees you coming, flicks a switch at the back of the Android, and darts off into the crowd. A whirring sound comes from the Android. It turns towards a man studying its arm and smashes him across the face with a powerful blow! Screams break out and the Android goes berserk, charging into the crowd, arms flailing. Will you pursue Utoshski (turn to **387**), or is your first duty to save the visitors from the mad Android (turn to **62**)?

426

Like a true hero, you grasp the bottle between your hands and try to smother the explosion. But the bottle is boiling-hot! You scream in pain as it burns your hands badly. You must lose 2 *SKILL* points and must now decide whether to fling the bottle through an open window (turn to **269** – but you need not lose another *SKILL* point), or rush off to look for a fire-extinguisher (turn to **89**).

427

You quietly slip into the Colonel's office and find the Macro Brain leafing through files. After your last encounter with the Macro Brain, you devised what you hope will be the perfect weapon against him, an Alpha-wave Emitter. You draw it from your Accessory Belt and set it going. If your theory is correct, generating alpha waves on such a highly developed mind will cause acute mental anguish – perhaps even epileptic fits, in such a sensitive subject. The Macro Brain clutches at his ears and spins round to face you. *'Aaarghh!'* he cries, clutching his ears with his hands. 'Crusader! It is you! If this is one of your devices, switch it off!' You smile at his obvious discomfort. You will switch it off if he tells you all he knows about the F.E.A.R. meeting which is to take place soon. The Alpha-wave Emitter is agonizing for him. 'All right! All right!' he agrees. The meeting is due to take place at a Chinese laundry, tomorrow. But that is all I know. Now switch that damn thing off!' You switch off your device and pin the Macro Brain's arms behind his back. You march him out into the courtyard, and the sight of your hostage ends the battle quickly. The F.E.A.R. troops surrender to the army. You may add 6 Hero Points for capturing the Macro Brain. Now you can return to town. Turn to **311**.

428

You resume your shopping-tour downtown. Will you make for 'Verging Records' to go and have a look at what new albums have come out recently (turn to **189**), or will you have a look in the window of Epiphany's, the famous jeweller's (turn to **300**)?

429

What can you get him? An apple? A bottle of whisky? A new tie? You decide to go for something a little more imaginative. Do you want to head downstairs to the Book Department (turn to **42**) or upstairs to the Games Department (turn to **355**)?

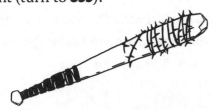

430

Some time later, things begin to happen. One of the jets is evidently ready and is being prepared for a flight. Six figures, dressed in heavy coats with turned-up collars, appear and get on board. Although you cannot make out any of their faces, one figure stands out as being much bulkier than the rest. His coat is an unnatural fit, bulging at all the wrong places. As he steps into the aircraft, the clang of metal on metal confirms your suspicions. Feet of steel! It is the Titanium Cyborg! Quickly you find a hiding-place and change into the Silver Crusader. But just as quickly, the jet is leaving the hangar and taxiing up the runway! What is your power:

Super Strength ?	Turn to **87**
Energy Blast?	Turn to **330**
Other?	Turn to **249**

431

You may award yourself 2 Hero Points for defeating Mustapha Kareem, alias the Mummy, The curator, needless to say, is incredulous when you explain what happened; Kareem had been with him for eleven years. Turn to **276**.

432

As the young starlet picks herself up and thanks you, the Serpent moans and pleads for mercy. He can offer you some information and wants to do a deal. He will tell you what he knows if you will release him. But you have sworn to uphold justice and can agree to no such deal. You explain that you can only suggest that helping you by relating this information may make the judge a little easier on him. Reluctantly he agrees. He tells you two pieces of information. First of all, you learn that the Creature of Carnage is in fact Illya Karpov, a known agent of F.E.A.R. Also he has heard that there will be an assassination attempt on the life of the President when he visits Titan City. The killer will be hiding on the roof of the Regent Hotel. If you decide to watch the President's arrival, add 100 to the reference you are on when you arrive to apprehend the assassin. You may add 2 *LUCK* points for this information. After you have handed him over to the police, turn to **79**. You may add 2 Hero Points for rescuing Lola Manche.

433

The Ringmaster pleads with you not to hand him over to the police; he has no wish to spend any more time in jail. In desperation he gives you a clue, which may or may not be useful. He tells you that the Ice Queen, in the disguise of her alter ego, Sylvia Frost, has bought the Titan abattoir. If you come across evidence of the Ice Queen's activities, deduct 20 from the reference you are on at the time and turn to this new reference. You may add 1 *LUCK* point for this information. The Ringmaster is hopeful that you will release him for telling you this news. Of course you are not willing to bargain with the man. You hand him over to the police and may award yourself 3 Hero Points. Now turn to **148**.

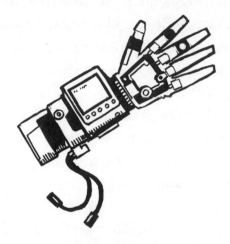

434

You manage to push through the crowd and you see a man's body slumped on the ground lying in a pool of blood. His head hangs at an unnatural angle. Judging from his clothes, he was a wealthy man, and a brown hide briefcase with gold fastenings lies by his side. But by now the police cordon is forcing you, along with the other onlookers, away from the scene. Turn to **181**.

435

'Lafayette! Get in here *at once!*' No sooner had you stepped through the office door than Jonah Whyte's booming voice summoned you. You creep into his office, mumbling scanty excuses for being late yet again. 'Enough!' he yells. 'What do you think we are running here? A charity? Do you suppose I should be grateful that you even grace us with your presence? Very noble of you indeed to even bother coming in at all! *Well,* I tell you what. I'm feeling kind today. You can have the rest of the day off. *Without pay!* And if you're not in first thing tomorrow morning, you can start looking for another job!' You slink out of his office with your tail between your legs. How can you tell him what you've been doing? And now you've been suspended for a day. Where will you go? Will you spend the day at Wisneyland, the amusement park (turn to **15**), or will you go downtown to do some shopping (turn to **202**)?

436

You leap aside to avoid being bowled over by the huge frozen weight. Quick as a flash, the Ice Queen is upon you! You must fight her:

ICE QUEEN   *SKILL 7*   *STAMINA 8*

The Ice Queen's touch is dangerous. Each time she lands a blow on you, its effect will be to freeze part of your body.

You must deduct 1 *SKILL* point for each successful attack she makes on you. You will not regain this *SKILL* until the next time you gain *STAMINA* points. If you defeat the Ice Queen, turn to **241**.

437

You leap on the leader and grapple with him on the floor. Although you have separated him from his test-tube rack, the Alchemist still has in his hand a tube of nerve-gas. While you fight him, you must take special care that he is not able to break the tube or else the innocent citizens – not to mention *you* – may be harmed. In view of this precaution, you must deduct 2 points from your Attack Strength during the struggle:

First ALCHEMIST   *SKILL 8*   *STAMINA 6*

If the Alchemist should inflict a hit on you, you must *Test your Luck*. If you are Lucky, continue as normal. If you are Unlucky, you must turn immediately to **28**. If you defeat the Alchemist you may go for the others (turn to **354**).

438

You make your way home and spend the rest of the night relaxing in front of the TV after the day's excitement. You may add 6 *STAMINA* points for the rest. The next morning you leave for work early. You travel by bus. As the bus enters Radd Square, you notice a disturbed crowd in the centre of the square. Something is happening! At that very moment, your Crimewatch sounds! You hold it to your ear and hear its message: *'COWFIELD DAIRY.' FAST.* Quickly you get off the bus. Will you investigate the disturbance in Radd Square (turn to **201**), or will you follow your Crimewatch's instructions and head towards Cowfield Dairy, two blocks away (turn to **369**)?

439

The Rotating Room is a huge barrel on its side which tumbles over and over. The people inside try desperately to walk forward at the same speed as it rotates in order to keep their footing; walking too fast or too slow means they fall over. There are three people inside as you enter and they are happy to leave at your request. Keeping your footing, you examine the inside and find a delicate key which has become stuck to the surface in a piece of chewing-gum. You decide to take it for examination. Turn to **37**.

440

The police are amazed. Single-handedly you have defeated the most dangerous association of criminals known to the world! And the extent of their dastardly plans soon becomes clear. Utoshski had developed a transmitting computer centre which was capable of overriding transmissions from the Pentagon to the US 'Star Wars' satellite orbiting the earth. He was able completely to control the super weapons on board the satellite, capable of decimating an entire city at the push of a button. His objective was the domination of the civilized countries of the world.

But you have foiled his plan. The Pentagon security codes can be changed almost immediately. And the Titanium Cyborg will be closely guarded for the rest of his life. You have earned 10 Hero Points for this victory. You can honestly say that you have saved the world from F.E.A.R. itself!

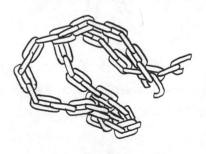

You have saved the world from F.E.A.R itself!

HOW TO BATTLE THE SUPER-VILLAINS OF TITAN CITY

In *Appointment with F.E.A.R.,* YOU will become the Silver Crusader, a superhero with unusual powers, dedicated to saving the citizens of Titan City from crime. You will come across robberies, kidnappings and destruction – crimes committed by a host of super-villains. You must also find out where the fateful meeting between the heads of F.E.A.R. (the Federation of Euro-American Rebels) is due to take place and capture Vladimir Utoshski, otherwise known as the Titanium Cyborg, F.E.A.R.'s leader.

You do not have only your super powers to aid you. Through your Crimewatch your friend and informant Gerry the Grass will alert you to crimes even before they are committed, and you can keep in touch with the police. And as you fight and overcome villains of the underworld, you will discover clues. Some clues will enable you to locate arch-criminals and arrest them; others will give you information on the whereabouts of the secret F.E.A.R. meeting.

You begin the adventure with a choice of four super powers. With *Super Strength,* you are powerful and have the ability to fly. *Psi-Powers* enable you to read minds and influence objects by brain-power alone. *ETS* (Enhanced

Technological Skill) provides you with a variety of devices and gadgets which you carry round in your Accessory Belt. If you choose *Energy Blast,* you can summon up a bolt of energy and project it from your fingertips. Depending on which power you choose, the solution to the book (finding the location of the F.E. A.R. meeting) will be different. Once you have solved it with one power, you can try it again with another.

And you may also monitor your success with your Hero Points score. When you overcome super-villains, you will be awarded Hero Points to allow you to compare the success of one adventure with another.

Because of these new features, the rules to *Appointment with F.E.A.R.* differ a little from other Fighting Fantasy Gamebooks. Combat is basically the same, but you will find several new sections in the following rules.

Before setting off to fight the super-villains of Titan City, you must first determine your own *SKILL, STAMINA* and *LUCK* scores by rolling dice as described below. On pages 266–267 there is an *Adventure Sheet* which you may use to record the details of your adventure. You are advised either to make records on the *Adventure Sheet* in pencil or to take photocopies of the page to use in future adventures.

SKILL, STAMINA AND LUCK

- Roll one die. Add 6 to this number and enter the total in the *SKILL* box on the *Adventure Sheet*. The exception to this is if you have *Super Strength,* in which case you will start with an automatic *SKILL* score of 13.
- Roll two dice. Add 12 to the number rolled and enter the total in the *STAMINA* box.
- There is also a *LUCK* box. Roll one die and add 6 to the number rolled. Enter this total in the *LUCK* box.

For reasons that will be explained below, *SKILL, STAMINA* and *LUCK* scores change constantly during an adventure. You must keep an accurate record of these scores and for this reason you are advised either to write small in the boxes or to keep an eraser handy. But never rub out your *Initial* scores. Although you may be awarded additional *SKILL, STAMINA* and *LUCK* points, these totals may never exceed your *Initial* scores.

Your *SKILL* score reflects both fighting and problem-solving skills; the higher your *SKILL* score the better. Your *STAMINA* score reflects your general constitution, your will to survive, your determination and overall fitness; the higher your *STAMINA* score, the longer you will be able to survive. Your *LUCK* score indicates how naturally lucky a person you are.

BATTLES

You will often come across pages in the book which instruct you to fight a villain of some sort. If so, you must resolve the combat as described below.

First record the villain's *SKILL* and *STAMINA* scores in the first vacant 'Villain Encounter Box' on your *Adventure Sheet*. The scores for each villain are given in the book each time you have an encounter.

Unlike other Fighting Fantasy Gamebooks, you may not *kill* the criminals you are fighting. As a sworn upholder of justice, you may not take the life of a super-villain, no matter how evil he or she may be. But *they* will be attempting to kill *you!* If you manage to reduce the *STAMINA* score of a criminal to zero, you have killed him and must lose 1 Hero Point as a result. When a criminal has been reduced to 1 or 2 *STAMINA* points, he will surrender himself to you.

The sequence of combat is then:

1. Roll two dice once for the criminal. Add his *SKILL* score. This total is the criminal's Attack Strength.
2. Roll two dice once for yourself. Add your own current *SKILL* score. This total is your Attack Strength.

3. If your Attack Strength is higher than his, you have landed a blow: proceed to step 4. If the criminal's Attack Strength is higher than yours, he has landed a blow on you: proceed to step 5. If both Attack Strengths are equal, you have avoided each other's blows: start the next Attack Round from step 1 above.

4. You have landed a blow on the criminal, so subtract 2 points from his *STAMINA* score. You may use your *LUCK* here to do additional damage (see over).

5. The criminal has landed a blow on you, so subtract 2 points from your *STAMINA* score. Again, you may use *LUCK* at this stage (see over).

6. Make the appropriate adjustments to either the criminal's or your own *STAMINA* scores, and to your *LUCK* score (if you used *LUCK*).

7. Begin the next Attack Round (repeat steps 1–6). This sequence continues until the *STAMINA* score of the criminal has been reduced to 2 or less *or* your own *STAMINA* has been reduced to zero. A criminal with a *STAMINA* of 2 or 1 is semi-conscious and will give himself up. A *STAMINA* score of zero (for you or the criminal) is equivalent to death. If you kill a criminal, you must lose 1 Hero Point, so be careful about this and use your *LUCK* when appropriate.

LUCK

At various times during your adventure, either in battles or when you come across situations in which you could be either lucky or unlucky (details of these are given on the pages themselves), you may call on your *LUCK* to make the outcome more favourable. But beware! Using *LUCK* is a risky business and if you are unlucky, the results could be disastrous.

The procedure for using your *LUCK* is as follows: roll two dice. If the number rolled is equal to or less than your current *LUCK* score, you have been Lucky and the result will go in your favour. If the number rolled is higher than your current *LUCK* score, you have been Unlucky and will be penalized.

This procedure is known as *Testing your Luck.* Each time you *Test your Luck,* you must subtract 1 point from your current *LUCK* score. Thus you will soon realize that the more you rely on your *LUCK,* the more risky this will become.

USING LUCK IN BATTLES

On certain pages of the book you will be told to *Test your Luck,* and will be told the consequences of being Lucky or

Unlucky. However, in battles, you always have the option of using your *LUCK* either to inflict a more serious blow on the criminal you have just hit, or to minimize the effects of a blow the criminal has just inflicted on you.

If you have just landed a blow on the criminal, you may *Test your Luck* as described above. If you are Lucky, you have landed a severe blow and may subtract an *extra 2* points from the criminal's *STAMINA* score. If you are Unlucky, however, the blow glanced off and you must restore 1 point to the criminal's *STAMINA* (i.e. instead of inflicting 2 points of damage, you have inflicted only 1).

If the criminal has just hit you, you may *Test your Luck* to try to minimize the effects. If you are Lucky, you have managed to avoid the full force of the blow. Restore 1 point of *STAMINA* (i.e. instead of taking 2 points of damage, you take only 1). If you are Unlucky, you have taken a more serious blow and must subtract 1 extra *STAMINA* point from your score.

Remember that each time you *Test your Luck* you must subtract 1 point from your own *LUCK* score.

RESTORING SKILL, STAMINA AND LUCK

Instructions for restoring your *SKILL*, *STAMINA* and *LUCK* scores will be given in the pages of the book as appropriate, *STAMINA* will be restored when you rest at home in the evening, *STAMINA* bonuses are difficult to come by, so be careful! *LUCK* points will be gained when you find some clues.

HERO POINTS

As you defeat super-villains and solve crimes, you will be awarded Hero Points, to be recorded on your *Adventure Sheet*. Hero Points have nothing to do with your main objective, which is to locate the secret F.E.A.R. meeting and capture Vladimir Utoshski, the Titanium Cyborg. Hero Points are a measure of how successful you have been in your adventure. Each time you go through the book, record your Hero Points score and compare each adventure with previous ones. As you will find, if you try a different super power, the solution to the book will be different, so you can rate your own performances with each of the four powers.

CLUES

Whichever super power you begin the game with, you will have knowledge of two clues which will help you trace and capture Titan City's criminals. Indeed, you will not be able to find some of the villains without knowledge of the appropriate clues.

In fact there are two types of clue. Some relate to the villains and their crimes – the ones you start with are of this type. Others relate to the secret F.E.A.R. meeting. Without finding the necessary clues to the meeting, you will never be able to prevent it, with disastrous results for Titan City! So bear in mind that you must find these F.E.A.R. clues, and remember also that, when you try the adventure using a different super power, the F.E.A.R. clues that you need will be held by different villains!

ADVENTURE SHEET

SKILL

STAMINA

LUCK

CLUES

SUPER POWER

HERO POINTS

VILLAIN ENCOUNTERS

SKILL
STAMINA

SKILL
STAMINA

SKILL
STAMINA

SKILL
STAMINA

SKILL
STAMINA

SKILL
STAMINA

SKILL
STAMINA

SKILL
STAMINA

SKILL
STAMINA

SKILL
STAMINA

SKILL
STAMINA

SKILL
STAMINA

ADVENTURE SHEET

SKILL

STAMINA

LUCK

CLUES

SUPER POWER

HERO POINTS

VILLAIN ENCOUNTERS

SKILL

STAMINA

SKILL

STAMINA

SKILL

STAMINA

SKILL

STAMINA

SKILL

STAMINA

SKILL

STAMINA

SKILL

STAMINA

SKILL

STAMINA

SKILL

STAMINA

SKILL

STAMINA

SKILL

STAMINA

SKILL

STAMINA

YOU ARE THE HERO

FIGHTING FANTASY

COLLECT THEM ALL, BRAVE ADVENTURER!